She could ▯
with Ben in t▯

'When I'm a secret agent, will I be able to tell you and Mummy?'

'You'll pretend you're something else,' Ben answered seriously. 'But we'll probably guess. The fast cars and women will give it away.'

'Fast cars.' Jamie sounded thoughtful. 'Like yours?'

'Much better.' Amusement made Ben's deep voice almost husky. 'And probably red.'

'I like red. Do secret agents have to work all the time, like you?'

'Lots of people have to work funny hours like Mummy and me.'

'Does Mummy like being a doctor?' Claire lingered, interested in Ben's reply.

'You'll have to ask Mummy,' he said.

Kids…one of life's joys, one of life's treasures.
Kisses…of warmth, kisses of passion, kisses from mothers and kisses from lovers.
In *Kids & Kisses*…every story has it all.

A New Zealand doctor with restless feet, **Helen Shelton** has lived and worked in Britain, and travelled widely. Married to an Australian she met while on safari in Africa, she recently moved to Sydney, where they plan to settle for a little while at least. She has always been an enthusiastic reader and writer, and inspiration for the background for her medical romances comes directly from her own experiences working in hospitals in several countries around the world.

Recent titles by the same author:

A SURGEON'S SEARCH
POPPY'S PASSION

A MATTER OF PRACTICE

BY
HELEN SHELTON

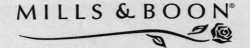

MILLS & BOON®

First published in Great Britain 1998
Harlequin Mills & Boon Limited,
Eton House, 18-24 Paradise Road, Richmond, Surrey TW9 1SR

© Poppytech Ltd 1998

ISBN 0 263 81034 8

Set in Times Roman 10½ on 11 pt.
03-9807-54317-D

Printed and bound in Great Britain
by Mackays of Chatham PLC, Chatham

CHAPTER ONE

HURRYING downstairs, Claire trailed her hand along the underside ledge of the oak banister, wincing when she saw how much dust her fingers had collected. Housework hadn't been a priority lately but she made a mental note to make it one at the weekend if her on-call duties for the practice weren't too arduous. Even a few hours would make a difference, she reasoned, and the house badly needed it.

Wendy, her son Jamie's child-minder, was paid extra to help with chores while Jamie was at school but she wasn't an enthusiastic cleaner. Ruefully, Claire acknowledged that guilt about asking Wendy to do what she herself had once managed easily was mostly to blame for her lack of forcefulness when it came to discussing the issue with the younger woman. Besides, Wendy was excellent as far as the nannying side of her work went, Claire reminded herself. The best they'd ever employed—kind, likeable, friendly and happy to spend hours playing the complicated and mysterious games Jamie enjoyed.

Remembering the problems there'd been with previous nannies—the boyfriend troubles, the endless phone calls to Australia and the tiresomely inappropriate interest in Ben they'd each eventually developed—Claire grimaced. Since switching from part-time to full-time general practice two years ago she no longer had time for dramas like that and, telling herself that she should be quietly grateful for Wendy rather than accumulating complaints, she bent and retrieved her bulging briefcase from the rack by the front door and quickly flicked through its contents. She had a meeting about one of her patients in half an hour and she had to try and be at least semi-briefed.

'Jamie, hurry,' she called, hauling out a sheaf of papers and glancing through them, annoyed with herself for not having found time the night before. She'd been on call and had had to go out twice during the night, but with so much to catch up with she should have dragged herself out of bed an hour earlier than she had. 'Jamie? You're going to be late for school.'

'Coming.' Her son's high voice came from the kitchen behind her where she was confident he'd still be dawdling over his cornflakes. 'In a second.'

'We don't have a second,' she added absently, skimming the pages. 'It's Tuesday,' she called, more loudly now. 'Don't forget your football gear. I've left your shorts in the laundry.'

'I'm late, too.' Ben pressed an impersonal kiss to her cheek on his way past, enveloping her briefly in the familiar, faintly citrus scent of his aftershave. 'Claire, will you get the dry-cleaning today?' He frowned at her blank look. 'My new suit. It's been ten days.'

'Can't you get it yourself?' Her eyes widened as he swung away from her towards the door. 'It's my night to go to the university. I'll be late home.'

'I'll be later.' He opened the newly deadlocked front door, a recent purchase—along with an alarm—which their insurance company had insisted on after their second burglary in six months. The part of Chiswick where they lived was good—well established and prosperous—but prone lately to break-ins. 'Leave the suit till tomorrow, then—I'm at the college tonight.'

'But you can't be!' She stared at him, appalled by his reference to what she assumed was the Royal College of Surgeons. 'You're collecting Jamie after school.'

'Sorry. Can't do.' She watched him look out into the pale spring morning and saw the faint grimace that suggested it wasn't as warm as she'd hoped. 'Bill's away at that conference and I'm covering his list,' he said briskly before she could muster a protest, his dark hair brushing warm against her leg when he crouched to retrieve an umbrella from the rack beside her. 'I'm operating till five, then the wards will take another couple of hours so I'll have to go straight to dinner. It might go late. Don't wait up.'

She couldn't remember the last time she had, but there was no time for that now. 'Ben...what conference? What do you mean, straight to the college? I warned you last week that you'd have to collect Jamie today.' Inwardly she cursed herself for not going to his room to remind him when she'd come in from her calls the night before. 'You promised.'

'Sorry. Nothing I can do.' But the shrug of his broad shoulders beneath the immaculate fabric of his dark suit was more philosophical than regretful and she felt herself growing more tense. 'Ask Wendy. She won't mind collecting him.'

'Wendy's not here this week,' she snapped. Clearly Ben took even less interest in what happened within the household than she'd realised, and she'd assumed that was very little. 'Her mother's not well. She went up to York on Saturday to see her and she'll be away all week. And Tuesday is her afternoon off, anyway. She never covers Tuesdays.'

'I didn't know,' he said darkly. 'Come on, Claire. I haven't time for this. There must be someone who can babysit. What about your mother?'

'Normally, yes, but she's doing tomorrow after school and the weekend,' Claire protested. Ben would be away all weekend at a course for surgical fellowship trainees in Edinburgh and since she was on call Saturday and Sunday, likely to be called out at any time, she'd asked her mother to stay and supervise Jamie. 'She's not young any more,' she added. 'Jamie tires her even if she won't say anything. I can't ask her to do tonight as well. I've been able to make arrangements for the rest of the week but I didn't even try for tonight. You said you were free.'

'I was wrong.' Sparing her only the briefest look, he walked out—leaving Claire staring after him open-mouthed.

She swore. Angrily she shoved the papers back into her bag then hauled it off the table, wincing when it swung painfully against her calf as she hurried after him, furious that he seemed to have made up his mind to ignore her. 'Ben, this isn't fair. You promised—'

'There's nothing I can do.' He unlocked his Saab, then frowned at her. 'I've already said I'm sorry,' he said deeply, 'and I am. I didn't remember, and even if I had I wouldn't have realised it'd make a difference because I didn't know Wendy was away. It's hell at work this week—we've two surgeons on leave, Lisa was sick yesterday and I don't know if she'll be in today. I can't get off even for an hour.'

Claire tensed, a familiar coldness beginning to grip her insides. It wasn't the first time something like this had happened, but now, rushed and under strain herself—strain that she recognised was caused by knowing she was inadequately prepared both for her work that day and for her studies that evening, she wasn't going to make it easy for him. 'So I have to sort this out?'

'Be reasonable,' he said tightly, the abrupt switch in his expression from impatience to resignation suggesting that he'd sensed her mood. 'You're a GP. You have a lot more time than I—'

'I have no time,' she shouted, even more infuriated than usual by his easy assumption that her day was a blissfully gentle drift through her patient list. In common with most of the hospital consultants she encountered, Ben, despite being her husband and despite his clear dislike of the long hours she worked, never appeared to grasp the amount of work a general practitioner had to do. 'I do not have a second at the moment. I have meetings all morning for which I am horribly, *horribly* ill prepared, then my clinics and then I have to go to the university for my teaching session.'

'So skip it.' Ben shrugged, apparently not seeing any problem with that. 'Skip the teaching session.'

'So you can go to your stupid college's dinner?' she raged. 'My teaching is more important. I've already missed last month's two lectures because you couldn't come home when you'd said you would. You know how much I value this session. It's the only teaching I get these days and it's only two hours a fortnight.'

'I happen to be speaking at the *stupid* dinner,' he ground out, clearly too stung by her description of his evening at the college to have listened to her protests. 'Believe it or not, it's considered an honour to be asked. And it's too late to back out.'

'I don't care.' She was tired of giving in, bitterly tired, she realised. These days she seemed to do nothing else. Marriage was supposed to be give and take, but she was the one who seemed to do all the giving. He had a demanding job, yes—even more demanding than her own—she was prepared to admit, but that didn't make her work any less taxing.

'Tell them you've got laryngitis,' she hissed, following him all the way to the car so that she didn't have to shout and risk disturbing Jamie—or the neighbours, who were all, she acknowledged brutally, probably becoming immune to their rows. 'Think of something, Ben. We both know you can be inventive enough when you choose to be.'

She paused, waiting for that to sink in. 'At least you used to be,' she added bitterly. 'Lately, of course, I wouldn't know.'

Ben's expression darkened and the gaze that swung back to her was hard and glittering, and she registered dull satisfaction that her jibe had struck home.

'This isn't the time,' he growled, wrenching his car door open with a barely controlled force that betrayed his own anger. 'I'm attending the dinner. Arrange for Jamie to go to a friend's house after school. Call my secretary with the details and I'll pick him up after I've spoken. I'll get away as soon as I can, hopefully by nine. All right?'

'No. No, not all right.' She hated herself for sounding like a shrew but still couldn't help herself. The control she'd once prized herself on had worn itself to a thin layer which was easily pierced these days. 'I'm sick to death of this. When I went back to work full time you promised you'd help. It's been two years now and I still can't rely on you. Just because you don't like me working—'

'Quiet, Claire.' His hard gaze focused on something behind her. 'Later. Little pitchers.'

'Little pitchers…?' Claire whirled around, smoothing her expression before she faced Jamie who now stood on the top step watching them. Her heart clenched as she registered the quiet pallor that suggested he'd caught at least the tone of their conversation, and abruptly her anger subsided, leaving her drained and weary, aching with love for her son.

'Mummy…?'

'It's all right, darling. I'm coming now.'

'Bye, Jamie.' Ben's voice was deep and calm. 'See you later.'

Jamie looked faintly reassured. 'Bye, Daddy.'

Vague, dull frustration made Claire clench her fists when she heard the Saab start then accelerate away, but although she knew Ben was using Jamie's appearance to escape more discussion she was thankful he'd made an effort to conceal evidence of their disagreement from him.

'I'm ready, darling,' she said huskily. 'Got your boots?'

'In here.' He patted the fat satchel slung across his shoulders.

'Come on, then.' She bent and kissed the top of his sandy head, then directed him towards her Audi. 'Just let me set the alarm and lock up.'

When she joined him in the car he was already buckled up. Before she drove out onto the street she said carefully, 'How about going to Mitch's house after school? I'll call his mum and ask if you can stay for dinner. I can pick you up after university.'

'OK.' Jamie didn't look at her, his small hands clutching at the strap of his seat belt. 'If you want.'

'Don't you want?' She spared him another quick glance as she turned onto the leafy street. 'I thought you liked playing at Mitch's?'

'Did you?'

Claire's teeth bit into her lower lip, the loaded remark reminding her how like his father he was—not only in looks. 'Didn't Mitch get a great computer game for his birthday?'

'It's all right.' He lowered his head. 'Why are you cross with Daddy?'

'Oh, Jamie.' Stopped at traffic lights at the corner of Chiswick High Road, Claire allowed her eyes to close briefly. 'We were talking about how much Daddy works. And about how much I work too, I suppose. I thought he would be home tonight to look after you but he won't be. That's all. I'll ask Mitch's mother instead. There's nothing for you to worry about.'

But despite the confident sound of her reassurance she was no longer sure of that. She wasn't sure of anything any more, she reflected. Days like this tested her stamina to the full. 'Daddy's very busy at the moment. Some of the people he works with are away and he has to do all their work.'

'He told me,' Jamie remarked, and she looked at him

quickly, wondering that Ben had thought to tell Jamie yet, until this morning, not her. 'Lisa's sick.'

'Lisa?' Claire's gear change as the car surged away from the intersection was clumsy. Lisa was Ben's current registrar. It was her second term working with Ben, which meant she'd been with him almost a year now. A cool, very attractive blonde, Claire had found her cold and unfriendly on the few social occasions they'd met and perennially unhelpful when they'd had to speak professionally. Ben, though, seemed to like her. Lisa was an excellent surgeon, apparently, and the way he defended the other woman if Claire dared to voice any criticism suggested that he thought it was Claire who had the problem.

Personally, she remained unconvinced. Her own judgement was sound, she believed, while Ben's, normally astute, had been foiled by Lisa's doll-like looks and calculated charm.

And now that Jamie had mentioned the subject she remembered Ben saying something about her being unwell. She swerved to avoid a delivery van that suddenly braked ahead of her. 'I didn't know you'd met Lisa, darling.'

'We play on the swings when Daddy takes me to his office. She comes to McDonald's. She gives me her chips.'

Claire's hands clenched on the steering wheel. Neither Jamie nor Ben had ever mentioned spending time with Lisa outside working hours. 'When does Lisa come to McDonald's, Jamie?'

'When you're working.'

But she worked every third night and weekend so that was hardly reassuring. Claire frowned, her unease increasing. 'Who told you that Lisa was sick?'

'She did.' He activated the button that lowered his window, lifting his head as if smelling the cool, faintly rain-scented breeze that came in.

Trying to keep her voice casual, Claire said, 'When, darling?'

'Yesterday. On the telephone. She wanted to speak with Daddy but I answered.'

'Was this when I went out on my calls?'

'I don't know.' Jamie wound his window up again, falling silent, and—knowing that drawing attention again to the things he'd told her wouldn't help either of them Claire resisted the urge to question him further, forcing her concentration back to her driving as she negotiated the busy traffic approaching Hammersmith.

Ben hadn't been on call the night before, she found herself thinking. So why would Lisa have needed to phone him? It couldn't have been to warn him that she'd be away again today because this morning he'd said he didn't know if she'd be back.

When she pulled up outside Jamie's school she managed a pale smile, ruffling his hair gently as she turned to him. 'I'm sorry I've been so busy too, darling. I'm on call this weekend and Daddy's away in Scotland, but how about the one after that I take you somewhere special?'

'OK.' He smiled slightly. 'The dinosaur museum?'

'I'd love that.' On their last visit to the Natural History Museum in South Kensington a year earlier Jamie had been fascinated by the model dinosaurs on display and she remembered she'd promised him then that they'd visit again soon.

She straightened his tie affectionately. She'd ask Ben to come too, she vowed, wishing she could ignore the disquiet Jamie's revelations about Lisa had provoked. They'd make it a family outing, their first for months. 'See you tonight,' she said, leaning to open the door for him. 'I'll pick you up from Mitch's. Have a lovely day, darling.'

'Bye.' Scrambling out, Jamie lifted one hand to wave to two boys just ahead of him on the path who'd turned back to wait, then pushed the door shut and ran up to them.

Claire waited until he was inside the broad iron gates of the school before checking her mirrors and pulling out into the traffic again.

Ben wouldn't, she thought flatly, feeling sick now that she didn't have to try and conceal her thoughts from Jamie. Not Lisa. Would he...?

A sprinkling of rain scattered across the windscreen but instead of activating the wipers she found herself swerving the car sharply into the side of the road, not caring that the wheels grazed the gutter with a grating squeal as she braked. Then she sat for a while, staring blankly at the double-decker red bus that pulled into a stop just ahead of her.

He'd always been a highly sexed man, she acknowledged faintly, trying to stay rational. They used to make love every day, often more than once—even having Jamie hadn't changed that. But this last year...

She closed her eyes weakly. If he was involved with Lisa it would explain a lot, she thought dazedly. A lot about their own relationship. Moving herself from the bed they'd shared for most of their married life into one of the spare bedrooms had been her idea, admittedly— she hadn't wanted to wake him on the frequent occasions she was disturbed when on call, and equally she'd been too tired these last two years to be happy about being woken when he was on call—but she'd never denied him sex, not once. He'd simply stopped asking.

And the fighting...? She lowered her head onto arms she crossed on the steering-wheel and let out a soft groan. They'd argued in the past occasionally but never like this, never hateful unresolved arguments that lingered and continued and piled on top of each other each more resentful than the last.

Did he want a divorce? Was that why this was happening? Was he so unhappy with her, she wondered, that he no longer wanted to discuss their problems? And what about Lisa?

She stayed there, with lowered head, until a horn tooted. 'Clearway, love,' a good-natured voice shouted, and she looked up, managing an apologetic smile for the grinning passenger of a builder's van which had slowed next to her. 'Can't park there till after peak hour. Better move on or the coppers will have you.'

'Sorry,' Claire murmured weakly, returning his wave when she realised he wouldn't have heard her. Mechanically she started the Audi and pushed it into gear.

It didn't take long to reach St Paul's Hospital. A tattered and, rumour had it, doomed Victorian institution about fifteen minutes by car from the practice, it housed a large psychiatric unit and was the venue for her patient's case conference, scheduled to start in a couple of minutes.

But she'd only met her patient, Susan Drury, once, and that had been four months earlier, she reflected, unhappily aware of the paucity of her knowledge of Susan's history as she skimmed the notes she'd received the day before from the previous general practitioner—trying to keep her attention focused on that and only that as she made her way through the car park to the psychiatric department. The one time she'd seen her, Susan had been euphoric and acutely psychotic, convinced she could fly from the window of the third-floor flat she was in.

Unhappily, Claire's attempts to persuade her that she needed treatment had failed, forcing her to call in the police and start proceedings that had quickly had Susan admitted as an involuntary patient to St Paul's for emergency treatment.

From the notes, she saw that this was Susan's third hospital admission and that she'd first been diagnosed with a bipolar mood disorder—manic-depression—at age seventeen. Since then she'd had one other manic episode following a period of deep depression, although until this latest breakdown her mood had been relatively stable for several years.

Reaching the conference room where the meeting was due to start, Claire nodded at a few familiar faces, recognising two community psychiatric nurses and a social worker. She poured herself a strong coffee, before taking a battered wooden seat, determined to use the time before the start of the meeting to finish her reading.

The case conference was aimed at ensuring that all the health professionals involved in Susan's care understood their future role in helping to manage any problems that might arise.

The consultant psychiatrist supervising Susan spoke first, outlining treatment since admission, describing Susan's favourable response and announcing that she would be discharged the following Monday. 'Providing there's no descent into a major depression,' he qualified.

Claire asked what follow-up arrangements would be made from the medical point of view.

'A community-based psychiatric nurse will visit weekly and Susan will come to me at the end of three months,' he explained. 'If she's stable we'll revert to the nurse monthly and she'll come to you outside of that. If there're any problems call me.'

'Fine.' Claire made a note on her pad to that effect, she thought, but when she looked at it seconds later she was startled to see she'd merely written her husband's name several times over. She stared at the words disbelievingly, then folded the page hurriedly, trying to concentrate as one of the community's social workers outlined the arrangements being made for accommodation for Susan after her discharge.

The flat in which Claire had seen her had been owned by a boyfriend who had persuaded her to stop taking her medication—the major factor leading to her latest breakdown—but he'd lost interest in her and no longer wanted anything to do with her so she had nowhere to live. Her parents lived in Manchester, several hours north by train from London, but Susan's relationship with them was difficult and she wanted to stay in London. There was a room she could take in a halfway house designed for newly discharged patients for six weeks but then there would be a need for alternative accommodation, yet to be found.

Someone asked about work. 'Despite her first break-down she began studying European languages at university,' the social worker replied. 'But after her second admission she wasn't able to go back and at this stage still feels she wouldn't cope. I agree—she's too brittle at present. She's spent three years doing temporary office work and that's the sort of work she's going to look for again.'

The discussion continued, concluding with the psychiatrist announcing that he was 'cautiously optimistic' about Susan's future prospects. She was intelligent and insightful, he noted, and without the influence of her ex-boyfriend he was happy she'd now be compliant and take her medication, which meant that the worst peaks and lows of the mood swings that characterised her condition might be avoided.

When the meeting broke up Claire went to visit Susan. She hadn't seen her since the day of her admission and she regretted that. The thin, pale but quietly assured woman she found in the ward day room was a very different person to the loudly euphoric, flushed and singing woman she'd admitted weeks earlier.

She introduced herself but Susan remembered her. 'Hello,' she said quietly, nodding at Claire's request to join her. 'Thank you for your help when I was sick. I'm sorry if I wasn't appreciative at the time.'

'You weren't well,' Claire countered, remembering Susan's vigorous attempts to struggle free of her and the police in order to fly away.

They exchanged gentle smiles then talked for a short time about things that weren't very important—the weather, the hospital, the area—Claire pleased they were establishing a rapport that hopefully boded well for their future relationship.

Later when she arrived at the practice Claire found herself immediately diverted into the waiting-room, together with the other three partners and the rest of the practice staff, for their regular monthly meeting with the practice manager. Today he seemed determined to tackle the issue of cost-cutting and budgetary restraints, and the arguments and protests his suggestions received kept the discussion lively and a welcome distraction from the darkness of her own thoughts.

After that the partners met privately for half an hour and then, because she still had a few minutes before her first appointment, she joined David, one of the partners, for coffee in his office.

'Have you looked at the list of drugs they're asking us not to prescribe?' he complained, slumping into his chair as he scanned the printout their manager had given each of them, obviously aghast. 'I use at least half of these regularly.'

He drank his coffee in a few urgent gulps, then poured another from the jug they'd brought in and to Claire's puzzlement, she saw that his hands were shaking slightly. But, perhaps seeing her gaze, his expression stiffened, and he folded his hands away. 'If he thinks I'm going to change my prescribing habits,' he said quickly, 'he's mad.'

'They're only guidelines,' she suggested cautiously, perching on the edge of his desk and sipping her coffee as she studied her own list. David was exaggerating, she realised. The list was confined to expensive items, not ones she herself commonly used. 'And at this stage it's just for comment.'

'At *this* stage,' he repeated, his grimace suggesting he expected that to change. 'How did Ben enjoy La Cantina Friday night?'

Claire felt herself stiffen. With deliberate calm, as if the question was of absolute inconsequence, she said, 'La Cantina? The restaurant? You saw him?'

'Rebecca and I had dinner together,' he said jerkily, referring to his soon to be ex-wife. 'Sorting out the final details of the settlement.' His mouth tightened fractionally. 'Naturally she chose the most expensive restaurant in the area,' he continued, his bitterness ill-concealed, although, after hearing repeatedly about how his wife of five years had deserted him for a stockbroker it appeared she'd been having an affair with, Claire felt sympathetic.

'She saddled me with the bill even though that hotshot of a boyfriend of hers must make three times what I do,' David added. But his expression eased as he turned back to her carefully masked expression. 'Ben was with his registrar,' he continued. 'Lisa, isn't it?'

CHAPTER TWO

CLAIRE just managed a stiff nod. She wondered if she looked as pale as she felt.

David finished his drink then, when her gaze dropped involuntarily to his hands again, he picked up a folder from his desk as if to conceal the shaking she'd noticed earlier. 'Beautiful woman,' he said abruptly, his eyes glittering slightly now. 'Stunning.'

'She's a very good surgeon,' Claire contributed numbly.

'They seemed engrossed but I did say hello,' he told her. 'Did he tell you?'

'He…he might have mentioned something,' Claire lied. She gulped the rest of her drink and then stood shakily.

'Reward for hard work?' David ventured, still watching her. 'I suppose that's why he took her out?'

'He does that occasionally,' she managed, her cup clattering slightly in the saucer as she carried it towards the door. 'Time to earn a living,' she said brightly, hoping her tone sounded less forced to him than it did to her.

Her own hands shaking this time, she rinsed the cup in the tiny kitchen at the rear of the practice then took a few minutes to compose her expression and settle her agitated thoughts, before walking back to her office and greeting the two patients who'd arrived to see her. They were the parents of a child she'd recently diagnosed with leukaemia and she'd scheduled an hour for them for relationship counselling

Rachel had been an inpatient at the local hospital for

almost two weeks now and, although they all knew that there was at least an eighty per cent chance of her going into remission with initial chemotherapy, her parents' relationship, not strong before these problems, was even more strained now.

Fending off an unpleasant pang of distress at the irony of herself offering marital counselling to the pair at a time when her own marriage felt frighteningly less than secure, she began the session. At their early meetings she'd explored the broader issues in their conflict, encouraging them to see that in many ways their conflicts mirrored the conflicts their own parents had exhibited when they themselves were children. Today, remembering how worried Jamie had been by her argument with Ben and concerned by how Julie's and Victor's disputes might be affecting Rachel when she was so ill, she concentrated on tackling the superficial conflicts they were experiencing now.

By the end of the session they seemed to have made progress.

'I didn't mean it,' Victor conceded dully, lowering his head when his wife talked about how guilty she'd felt when he'd accused her of delaying too long before bringing Rachel to see Claire. 'I was angry with myself.'

For a man adroit at avoiding discussing his emotions it was a significant admission, and Julie's wide-eyed stare told Claire she realised it, too. 'But you shouldn't be angry,' Julie protested. 'It wasn't your fault.'

'Nobody's done anything wrong,' Claire said gently. 'If Rachel was my daughter I know I wouldn't have taken her to a doctor any earlier than you did. It's normal for children to have a few bruises and be tired after school. You are both good parents.'

To Claire's delight the couple exchanged faintly shy smiles at that, the first smiles she'd seen between them, and when the session ended Victor helped Julie with her coat, his hands lingering a few seconds on her shoulders.

Pleased, because when they'd arrived they'd barely been speaking, Claire showed them out of the office, arranging to see them again later in the week.

It was one-thirty, half an hour before her afternoon clinic, but she had no appetite and so contented herself with a coffee and a couple of biscuits from the communal tin in the kitchen.

Afterwards she called Mitch's mother, who confirmed that she was happy for Jamie to go there after school, then Claire deliberately turned her attention to the large stack of paperwork and laboratory results in her in-tray.

Late that afternoon the practice's receptionist buzzed her to say that Ben's secretary was on the telephone. 'She wants to know what the arrangements are for Jamie for the evening.'

'Tell her it's organised,' Claire said stiffly. In the middle of a busy clinic—and irritated that Ben hadn't bothered to phone himself—she didn't want to take the call. It would only have taken him a few seconds, she told herself, but clearly he didn't think the issue of his son's care warranted his personal attention. Then, conceding that she was allowing her bitterness about the reasons why he might be preoccupied to overcome common courtesy, she added tightly, 'Please thank her for calling but tell her Ben doesn't have to do a thing. He's a free agent.'

As he obviously saw himself, she added stonily but silently. But, even if the thought made her shake, sooner or later she was going to have to confront him, she acknowledged. But when? And how?

She arrived home just after nine, noting with relief that Ben's car wasn't there. She needed time to think, she'd decided, still not sure whether to confront him about Lisa or else take the far more appealing coward's path and pretend nothing was amiss until the issue became more obvious.

At seven and a half, Jamie was too heavy for her to carry him easily. He'd gone to sleep in the car after they'd left Mitch's so she had to shake him gently awake. 'Home, darling,' she said softly, half tugging, half pushing him, still sleepy and protesting, inside and upstairs to bed.

Bending to kiss his forehead, she heard Ben's car outside. Hurrying now, she pulled Jamie's door shut and retreated along the hallway to her room.

She heard the front door open and close, then the sound of him walking to the kitchen. She sat tense and still on the edge of the bed, waiting, and a while later she heard his firm steps on the stairs and then a brief hesitation that made her heart thunder.

But he didn't knock, and seconds later she heard him moving towards the main bedroom and then there were sounds from the *en suite* attached to that room, followed by silence.

Claire opened her door quietly and crept to the main bathroom, locking the door softly behind her. For a few minutes she just stared at her strained expression in the bathroom mirror, before smearing her face with cleanser and tissuing it off with trembling hands.

She overslept, waking just before seven instead of her usual six-fifteen. From the state of the bathroom—floor strewn with damp towels, a small pair of striped pyjamas carelessly discarded beside the shower and toothpaste all over the basin—she deduced that Jamie must already be up, and when she ventured downstairs after dressing she could hear him talking with Ben in the kitchen.

She paused by the table that held her briefcase, sorting through it to check she had everything she needed for the day.

'When I'm a secret agent, will I be able to tell you and Mummy?' she heard Jamie ask.

'You'll pretend you're something else,' Ben answered

seriously. 'But we'll probably guess. The fast cars and women will give it away.'

'Fast cars.' Jamie sounded thoughtful. 'Like yours?'

'Much better.' Amusement made Ben's deep voice almost husky. 'And probably red.'

'I like red. Do secret agents have to work all the time, like you?'

'Lots of people have to work funny hours like Mummy and me. Fire-fighters, the police, pilots—all sorts of people.'

'I think I might be a pilot, too,' said Jamie.

'Secret agents and pilots eat all their cornflakes,' Ben told him.

'I eat all my cornflakes.' Jamie giggled. 'One at a time.'

Claire smiled weakly—that was true enough. She tugged out a journal she'd intended to read before work and inspected the contents listed on the cover.

Jamie said, 'Don't you want me to be a doctor?'

'I want you to be whatever you want to be,' Ben's deep voice answered. 'Toast?'

'Is it good, being a doctor?'

'Most of the time. Jam or honey?'

'Jam, please.'

Claire slid the journal back into her bag then heard Jamie say, 'Does Mummy like being a doctor?' She lingered, interested in Ben's reply.

'You'll have to ask Mummy,' he said. 'But she seems to, yes.'

'Mummy loves being a doctor,' Claire said crisply, schooling her face into a neutral smile as she greeted them. 'All of the time.' She kissed Jamie's forehead. 'Morning, darling. I slept in. Why didn't anyone wake me?'

'Daddy told me I had to let you sleep.'

'Really?' Claire sent Ben a guarded look as she

spooned coffee into a mug. 'Aside from wanting to make me late for work, any particular reason?'

Ben's hard mouth tightened slightly at her jibe but he returned her regard steadily. 'You're looking more tired than usual lately.'

She topped her cup with hot water, stiffening. 'You've had more late nights.'

'I've never needed as much sleep.'

Silently Claire acknowledged the truth of that. Ben coped easily with sleep deprivation, rarely needing any more than five or six hours even when he wasn't working, while she needed a good eight to function properly, a luxury she rarely managed these days. 'Still, hardly a compliment, telling me I look tired.'

'It wasn't intended to be a compliment.' The air between them thickened. Leaving the rest of his toast uneaten he levered himself away from the table. 'I was stating a fact.'

'I'm perfectly fine.'

'I rather think the fact that you overslept disputes that,' he said coolly. He collected his briefcase from one of the other stools at the breakfast bar. 'I'm on call tonight so I'll be late.'

There's a surprise, she thought acidly, but, conscious of Jamie's presence, although he seemed preoccupied with his breakfast—oblivious, she hoped, to the undertones in his parents' conversation, she said merely, 'Fine.'

But it came out tight and short and Ben's narrowed eyes suggested he sensed her true sentiment. 'We're still two surgeons short,' he said tersely. 'There's nothing I can do.'

'I said, fine.' She stared back at him. 'If you're not here I don't have to cook. Jamie and I can have pizza.'

Jamie looked up from studying his cornflakes. 'Ham and pineapple.'

Claire wrinkled her nose at him. 'Yuk.'

'Half ham and pineapple, half vegetarian,' suggested Ben, his expression lightening as he contemplated his son. He kissed Claire's cheek impersonally then ruffled Jamie's hair on his way past, flashing him a quick grin. 'See you, 007.'

'Bye, Daddy.'

'I'll get your dry-cleaning today,' she said, taking her coffee and following him into the hall, a little taken aback by her sudden urge to appease him.

'Forget it,' he said coolly. 'Lisa was taking some things there last night and she said she'd pick the suit up for me.'

Claire froze. 'You told me she was sick.'

'Nothing major.' Ben lifted one shoulder casually as he opened the front door. 'She was back at work yesterday afternoon,' he drawled. 'Bye, Claire.'

Before she could say anything he'd pulled the door shut.

Because Ben was the surgeon on call for the day at the nearest hospital to the practice, Lisa, as his registrar, took all the referrals, and late that afternoon Claire had to call her about one of her patients. She noticed that her fingers had turned white where they gripped the telephone receiver as she waited for the younger woman to answer her page.

Her patient, a pleasant woman called Lily Thomas, had a fifteen-hour history of abdominal pain, which had now shifted to the right lower quadrant of her abdomen. Examining her, Claire found she was tender in that area with signs consistent with acute appendicitis.

Lisa, when she realised who she was speaking to, was cool to the point of abruptness. 'I'm extremely busy,' she said tersely. 'Please be succinct.'

Claire briefly described her patient's symptoms, hearing the edginess in her own voice. 'It looks like appendicitis,' she concluded. 'Shall I send her to A and E or would you prefer directly to a ward?'

'History of renal or bladder problems?'

'No.'

'Gynaecological disease?'

Claire gritted her teeth. 'None.'

'Pre- or post-menopausal?'

'She's sixty-six!' Claire took a deep breath. 'Look, it's classic appendicitis. I wouldn't be referring her to a surgical team if I didn't think that was appropriate.'

'There's no need to be offensive. I'm simply doing my job,' Lisa said coldly. 'If you knew how many misdirected referrals we receive from ill-informed general practitioners you'd understand—'

'I am not being offensive,' Claire grated. In fact, given the provocation and what the other woman might or might not be up to with her husband, she considered she'd been extremely professional. 'I'm merely trying to get proper care for my patient. And I appreciate your need for caution but this referral is not misdirected.'

She waited for the other woman to say something but when she remained silent Claire elected to call her bluff. It wasn't the first time Lisa had gone out of her way to be unhelpful to her, which made it especially ironic that Ben clearly thought so highly of her and that the male partners in Claire's practice frequently commented on how charming they found the younger woman.

'If you have difficulty accepting my word,' Claire added, 'I'll speak directly to Ben.'

'He's extremely busy,' the registrar answered stiffly. 'I doubt he'd talk to you.' But it seemed that Claire's threat had had some effect because she added grudgingly, 'Send Mrs Thomas to Accident and Emergency. I'll tell them to expect her. I'll examine her myself and decide if she needs admitting.'

'How kind.' Claire dumped the receiver back onto its cradle then lifted her eyes to the ceiling, before turning

her attention back to the referral note she was writing to
accompany her patient.

She hadn't planned to mention the incident to Ben but
he raised it first, coming to the door of the living-room
where she was perusing some of the practice's journals,
when he arrived home about ten.

'What's going on?' She registered that he hadn't at-
tempted even a token greeting. 'Lisa is still upset about
the way you spoke to her this afternoon.'

Claire bristled. 'What are you talking about?'

'I understand you're angry I couldn't collect Jamie
Tuesday night, but taking your anger out on my staff is
unreasonable.'

'But I didn't.' She dropped the journal she'd been
reading and surged to her feet, stunned by the unwar-
ranted attack. 'Whatever Lisa said—'

'She was on the verge of tears,' he ground out, eyes
cold. 'What the hell did you say to her?'

'I asked her to see my patient,' Claire exclaimed bitterly, seeing clearly where his loyalties lay. The thought
of their conversation driving the coldly collected Lisa to
tears was ludicrous, but obviously he was too besotted
with the younger woman to be able to view her with any
sort of objectivity. 'Entirely reasonable, I'd have
thought. Isn't that her job?'

'It's not her job to put up with abuse from angry GPs,'
he countered. 'Just because she asks a few simple questions—'

'It wasn't like that.'

'How was it, then?' Ben folded his arms and leaned
against the door frame, looking powerfully male and
deeply irritated. 'Come on, Claire. She asked if the problem might be gynaecological—'

'She implied I didn't know what I was doing.'

'She was trying to make sure the referral was appropriate.'

'She was being deliberately difficult.'

'Don't be ridiculous,' he snapped. 'Why would she do that?'

'You tell me.' Claire lowered her head, unable to sustain his glare, the words almost murmured. When there was silence she dared a look up. 'Well?'

His face changed, stilled. 'Claire…?'

'Was it appendicitis?' She spoke quickly, instinctively, frightened, wishing she hadn't been provocative. She didn't want to hear anything, she realised. She didn't want him to…tell her anything. Not yet. Not until she'd had time to calm herself, time to rehearse a response that would let her at least preserve some dignity. 'H-have you operated?'

'Lisa did.' His voice was lower now, calmer, more reasonable. 'Tonight. And it was appendicitis,' he conceded. 'But the fact that your diagnosis was correct doesn't mean Lisa wasn't entitled to question you. She's well qualified, experienced and good at her job, and it's part of that job to screen admissions.'

'I didn't object to the questions,' she said quietly, her attention superficially, for now, on the nondescript cover of the journal she'd discarded. 'I objected to the tone.'

'The tone?' He sounded tense. 'What tone?'

'Hostile,' Claire said stiffly. Slowly she lifted her head, forcing herself to meet his guarded expression, and keeping her own carefully emotionless. 'Unhelpful. Abrupt. Rude.'

'You're overreacting.'

'You're so predictable.' She was prepared to admit that she might be more sensitive with Lisa than with any of the other registrars although, given the circumstances, that was hardly surprising, but his refusal to believe her still stung. 'She goes out of her way to be difficult with me.'

'You're imagining it.'

'I'm imagining nothing.' Determined this time not to let their encounter deteriorate into a slanging match, she collected her journals. 'We've been though this a dozen times before. Ben, it's late…'

He pushed the door shut and she tensed when it closed with a click that struck her as faintly menacing. 'It's not ten-thirty.'

'I'm tired.' She eyed him warily. Close to the door, she couldn't get it open unless he chose to move, and his expression suggested he'd be prepared to restrain her physically if she tried. 'As you so kindly pointed out this morning.'

'You're always tired.'

'I'm working hard.'

'Too hard.'

Her mouth dried. 'This isn't the time.'

'I'm not going to make an appointment to speak with my own wife,' he said tightly.

Claire's eyes widened at the unfairness of that. 'Coming from you, that's ironic,' she said bitterly. 'Considering how many hours you spend at that hospital.' And with Lisa, she wanted to storm, but, knowing the row and what else that could provoke she held her tongue.

'I want you to stop working,' he said stiffly. 'At least, working the way you have been. Go back to part time.'

'You want. *You* want.' She dumped the journals on the floor and swung around to confront him, arms folded, abruptly furious. 'It's always what you want, Ben. Never me, never what I want. Well, I want to work, properly, full time. Like this. Believe it or not, I love what I do. I get satisfaction from caring full time for my patients.'

'Are you trying to tell me you're happy?' he demanded. 'When's the last time we had a weekend together? When's the last time you spent a whole day with Jamie?'

'I enjoy my work,' she stormed, refusing to give him the satisfaction of seeing her concerns about the inroads her job made into her personal time. 'And since when have you been worried about us spending time together?

I was free last weekend, all except Saturday morning clinic, and I was here, with Jamie, half of Saturday and all day Sunday. Where were you?'

'At the hospital,' he ground out.

Remembering where David had seen him on Friday night, she said acidly, '*All* weekend?'

'*All* weekend.' His dark eyes narrowed at the scepticism she made little effort to conceal. 'I told you we're short-staffed at the moment. And this isn't about me, Claire. This is about you. You're tired. You've lost weight and you look anaemic. You're wearing yourself out. Working like this isn't good for you. Why can't you admit that? It's too tough for you.'

'Only because I get no support from you,' she said bitterly. 'If you once tried to see things from my point of view—'

'If I, nothing.' Ben's face closed. 'I don't want you working like this.'

'What a revelation,' she raged, stabbing her forehead with the heel of her hand. 'I'd never have guessed.'

'It's not as if we need the money.'

'The money's got nothing to do with it.'

'Jamie needs his mother.'

'Jamie goes to school.'

'Only till three.'

'What about my training? What about the years I spent, studying, to get where I am now? What about the fact that I'm good at my job and I'm needed?'

'You're needed here, too.' He waited then continued, more conciliatory now, 'Be reasonable. I'm not asking you to stop working altogether. Go back to part time. Thirty, forty hours, if you must. But not like this. Not on call every third night. It's taking too much out of you.'

'My hours are shorter than yours.'

'We're talking about you.' He was quiet now, but no

less determined. 'If you like, I'll talk to Warren—make it plain—'

'Don't you dare.' She glared at him. Warren, the senior partner—although they no longer used that term—in the practice, had coached the rugby team Ben had played for at university, and the two men had remained friends over the intervening years and frequently met socially.

She already knew that Warren, who had no qualms about working every conceivable hour himself, had had reservations about her taking on the patient load she had. But she'd talked him out of those reservations. Her predecessor at the practice had been an old-fashioned GP—hard-working, dedicated, no family life to speak of. And, while Claire hadn't wanted to sacrifice her own family time, she'd hoped that by managing the list more efficiently she could clear herself some spare hours, without having to resort to off-loading her patients onto the others who already worked very hard.

And she was managing, she was genuinely convinced of that. And not only managing, but improving the service the practice offered. That success, and the satisfaction expressed by her patients, was addictive. Why should she give that up? Ben was exaggerating. She felt tired from time to time, yes, but everybody—with the possible exception of Ben, who seemed invincible—felt tired at times. She might have lost a pound or two but that was hardly significant, and his accusation that she looked anaemic was ridiculous.

In truth, she suspected, the strain she did feel came more from her anxieties about their relationship than from the pressure of work. And, leaving aside all of that—her work, her tiredness, his inane demand that she sit at home for him—the essence of their problems was him. And Lisa.

But she didn't want to think about that.

'My career is important to me,' she said shakily. 'Very important. Just like yours is to you. And Jamie's a social child who's perfectly happy with the situation, you know that. If he wasn't, I'd think again.'

'What about having another baby?'

Claire felt herself pale. 'What?'

'You heard.'

'Another…baby?' She stared at him, stunned, still not sure she'd heard him say the words.

But his hard expression and unflinching regard confirmed that she had. 'Why not?'

'Because…' She lifted her hands, unsure. 'Because… I don't know. I would like another child, yes, but I didn't think…You've never said…'

'I'm saying now.'

'I don't know.' She backed away, dry mouthed, confused. 'I don't understand.'

'It's not complicated,' he said heavily, and she saw that her bemusement had made him impatient.

'But we haven't…' And then she stopped, blushing furiously. 'We, I mean you…that is, we haven't…not in months.'

His eyes darkened fractionally. 'That's easily remedied.'

'No.' She held out her hand as if to fend him off, which was ridiculous, she registered faintly, because he hadn't moved. He only felt closer, frighteningly close.

'You used to say you wanted two at least.'

'Yes. Once.' She shook her head vaguely. 'And in some ways I still do, I think, but…things have changed,' she added huskily.

'You mean you went back to work.' His face hardened. 'Stop, Claire. Let's have another baby.'

'No.' She moved further away, reeling, still confused, wondering how she could reconcile this with her suspicions about his involvement with Lisa. Was he saying that a baby would bring him back to her, Claire? But did he really want that? Now, lately, like this, she didn't even know if that was what *she* wanted. Certainly not if it was only for the sake of another child. 'Ben...a baby...a baby won't help.'

'You're wrong.' He looked very sure. 'It's the right time for another one.'

'I...can't.' This was too much. Too much now. She couldn't think. With trembling hands, she gathered her journals again, holding them across her chest defensively as she made for the opposite side of the room and the other door which led to the kitchen.

'Wait.' At his command she froze, tensing as his hand closed around her arm. For the first time in a very long time he stepped towards her and she felt his breath at her forehead, the brief remembered touch of his mouth at her hair. 'Come to bed.'

'No.' With legs shaking and feeling weak, she wrenched herself away. 'No, Ben. Not now.' Dully registering the irony of his demand at this time, when she'd craved his touch for months, she took a step backward. Now, needing to think and remembering how he could overwhelm her, sex with Ben was the last thing in the world she could cope with. 'Please, no.'

His face hardened and the grip on her arm tightened but she twisted away. He didn't come after her. 'I won't beg,' he said darkly.

'I don't want you to beg,' she cried. 'I want you to leave me alone.' She ran through the kitchen and clumsily up the stairs, frightened that he would follow her—but when she reached her room she realised he hadn't.

Torn between relief, the panic that had gripped her downstairs and now the absurd, crazy urge to burst into hysterical laughter, she sank slowly onto the bed and lowered her head into her hands.

CHAPTER THREE

BEN had already gone when Claire got up the next morning.

Morning clinic was busy as always, but out on her calls in the afternoon—now that her head had cleared slightly after the confusion of the night before—she found time to think. Returning to the surgery in the late afternoon, she realised she'd worked out at least some idea of where to go with Ben.

She didn't know beyond doubt that he was involved with Lisa but, whether he was or not, she had no choice, she realised. If her feelings for Ben had changed—and trying to analyse her emotions had become confusingly difficult—there was still Jamie to consider. And the fact that Ben had asked her to have another baby had to mean that despite everything, he was still prepared to try and make their marriage work.

She paused, catching her lower lip between her teeth nervously as she considered the alternatives. For, disturbingly, his suggestion might merely mean that he was bored with his mistress. Perhaps he'd decided that telling her that his wife was pregnant would be a way of escaping the relationship?

Claire rested her forehead on her clenched fists. Ben was nothing if not decisive, she told herself, finding comfort in that. That last idea made little sense because, in truth, if Lisa bored him she suspected he'd have little difficulty walking away.

More disturbing, she realised, was the thought that Lisa might merely have told him she didn't want a child. Ben was strongly paternal—it was entirely possible his

mistress's refusal to have his child might drive him away
from her.

Whatever the reason, she reminded herself again, the
fact that Ben wanted her to have another baby had to
mean he wasn't planning to leave her for the younger
woman, at least not immediately. And that gave her
something to work with.

Julie Bright arrived without her husband, Victor, for
her afternoon counselling session. 'One of his best me-
chanics is away today so he has to help out in the work-
shop,' she told Claire, 'but I still wanted to come.' Without Victor, Claire found Julie much less guarded. 'We've
been talking a lot,' she said shyly, obviously pleased
about it.

Claire concentrated on working towards a stage where
Julie, in total contrast with her own inability to analyse
her feelings, could work towards an honest understanding of her feelings for her husband. 'Are you finding
these sessions helpful?'

'Oh, yes.' Julie seemed surprised by the question. 'Of
course.'

'Why?'

'Because…they've started him talking about the way
he feels,' Julie said slowly. 'And he's never done that
before—not to me. He's like my father that way.'

Claire understood how remote Julie's father had been
from an earlier session. Now she concentrated on Victor.
'Are you surprised by what he's saying?'

'I'm surprised by how differently we see things.'
When Claire waited, Julie tilted her head. 'It probably
sounds strange, but sometimes I think he thinks that he's
supposed to fix everything all the time, even things he
can't possibly fix. I mean, like me finding it stressful at
work or like Rachel being sick. And it's when there are
things happening that he can't fix that he seems to get
most frustrated and, seeing him like that, I get angry and
that's when we fight most.'

Applauding her insight, Claire said, 'None of that sounds strange at all. Do you think Victor's work has anything to do with the way he reacts?'

'He's certainly used to fixing everything there,' Julie said slowly. 'Not just because he's a mechanic himself but because all the men working under him always come running to him the instant there's a problem with anything. He complains about it, but he likes it that way, really. He likes it that they couldn't manage without him.'

'Do you think that being used to solving problems at his work might be part of the reason he finds it so frustrating not to be able to solve them at home?'

'I suppose, but mostly I don't want him to solve anything,' Julie protested. 'I just want us to share things and be a comfort to each other.'

'Have you ever told him that?'

'Not in so many words...' She hesitated. 'He should know.'

'Things are not always so straightforward. You've already said that he seems to see things differently and you also said earlier that you get angry when you see him frustrated.'

'I do. I hate seeing him like that. I hate it when he's not totally in control.' Then, as if realising the significance of that comment, she caught her breath. 'Oh.' For a few minutes she stared blankly ahead, and when she focused again Claire could see that her gaze was dazed. 'I thought it was all his fault, but I've been so wrong,' she said thickly. 'It's not just that he himself thinks that he should fix things—deep down I think I've been expecting him to do more as well, even though I know he can't. I have to talk to him. I've been so awful. I have to explain...'

She swung forward slightly and collected her handbag, her movements jerky. 'I have to go,' she said quickly, standing. 'I have to explain everything.' She rushed ahead of Claire to the door. 'He's a lovely man,' she said huskily. 'It hasn't been easy lately. I've said some terrible things, but I do love him still.'

Claire's throat tightened and she wished she could be as confident as Julie, about her own feelings for Ben. 'That's a good thing to know,' she answered, for it was a huge step for Julie considering how things had been when she'd first started seeing the couple. In the beginning they'd made it sound as if Rachel was the only thing holding them together and that if it hadn't been for her illness they'd already be apart.

'Come together next week, if you can,' Claire said quickly, seeing what a hurry Julie was in now. 'I'll try and visit Rachel in hospital over the weekend or at least early next week.'

'She'd love that,' Julie told her absently, obviously distracted. 'She's in a room on her own and she gets bored. Thanks, Dr Marshall. I have to go.'

Claire was on call that evening, which meant covering the six and a half thousand patients the practice cared for. Whoever was on call ran a no-appointments short evening clinic between six and eight-thirty and afterwards took calls from home via an answering service and a bleeper.

Lights were on at the house, and instead of Jamie being at their neighbours as she'd arranged he was home with Ben. The two of them—Jamie still in school uniform, Ben changed out of his suit and into jeans and a casual blue shirt which made him look no less attractive but to her relief fractionally more approachable—were sprawled across the carpet in the living-room, studying a huge game board dotted with tiny soldiers and weaponry.

It was past Jamie's bedtime but as it was such a treat for him to have time like this with Ben she didn't mention it. She bent and kissed Jamie's forehead, nervously avoiding Ben's enigmatic regard, then wrinkled her nose at their game. 'Who's winning?'

'Daddy, of course.' Jamie sounded cheerful. 'But we've miles to go. Daddy always wins,' he confided. 'He says it improves my competit...competition...?'

'Competitiveness,' Claire supplied, smoothing her hair behind her ear as she straightened. 'And he won't always be able to beat you.' She looked at her husband, determined to act normally and pleasantly, but when she spoke, instead of a polite enquiry about his day, what came out was an unpleasantly sharp, 'You're early.'

His eyes darkened momentarily, suggesting he'd registered the unintentional dig, but she felt her breath flow again when he didn't comment on it. 'Supper's in the kitchen, if you haven't eaten.'

'I...I haven't. Thank you.' Unaccountably, she found herself blushing and from the almost imperceptible sharpening of his regard she saw that he'd noticed that and it interested him, and that made her flush deepen.

She turned quickly, almost clumsily, and left the room, knowing from the prickling at her back as she walked into the hall and towards the stairs that he was still watching her.

Unbuttoning her blouse in her room, Claire saw that her hands trembled slightly. Grimacing, she discarded the blouse and hauled a dark woollen sweater over her head, swiftly exchanging her heels and tights for thick socks and her work skirt for a pair of jeans. She tucked her on-call bleeper into her hip pocket then hesitated, staring doubtfully at her reflection in the full-length mirror attached to her wardrobe door.

After more than eight years of marriage the prospect of an hour or two spent with their husbands wouldn't turn many women into a bundle of nerves, she acknowledged grimly, but it certainly did her. While she looked superficially relaxed, the casualness of her clothes adding to the impression, her reflection reassured her that she wasn't the doubt-riddled teenager she felt inside. Her dark, almost black, straight, chin-length bobbed hair, determined, firm chin, straight nose and deceptively unlined pale skin, as well as the tight-pressed line of her mouth and the solemn wariness of her hazel eyes made her look every week of her age, she decided.

And while she knew that having Jamie hadn't altered her figure—slender and gently curved as it had ever been—the practical clothes she wore now did little other than hint at her shape.

Which was the way she wanted it, she told herself firmly, knowing that even if she'd owned a seductive outfit she wouldn't have been able to face Ben in it. That would seem too obvious. Too desperate, she added. Besides, she couldn't compete with Lisa for looks. Even from her more than faintly jaundiced view of the other woman, Lisa was unarguably, as David had phrased it, 'stunning'.

What she herself had was their past, Claire told herself, and Jamie. And, given that their son meant the world to Ben, that was a good start. And at least in jeans she could maintain a shell of self-confidence, even if that confidence was frighteningly thin.

She went slowly back down the stairs and met Ben's eyes with careful calm when they lifted to watch her, not stopping, this time, to watch them play but continuing to the kitchen.

In the fridge she found a cling-film covered plate of macaroni cheese that Ben must have made. That suggested he'd been home very early, she noted, wondering why. He regularly worked late, even when he wasn't on call, and had done so for years. Only perhaps it hadn't all been working, she registered dully. At least not lately.

While she waited for the microwave to signal that the food was hot she stared out of the window, the light from the kitchen casting a rectangle of sharp illumination onto the pale lawn outside. The gardener must have been in these last days, she decided, noting the short grass and the trimmed boarder around Jamie's swing. She smiled faintly, remembering how he used to spend hours swinging gently back and forth while she'd pottered about in the garden. Before she'd returned to work full time she'd maintained everything herself and there'd been no need to employ outside help.

Although Jamie had often tried to help, she remembered, her smile deepening, inevitably he'd ended up doing more damage than good, particularly when he'd turned his childishly chubby hands to weeding. But they'd had fun together.

These days she didn't have time to grow her own vegetables. She rarely even managed to cook properly and they bought most of their food ready-prepared from the Marks and Spencer's supermarket in the High Road.

After eating, she stacked her dishes into the dishwasher, then Jamie came and kissed her good-night. 'Daddy's going to read to me,' he confided in a whisper. 'OK?'

'OK.' She crouched to hug him. 'Make sure he doesn't skip any pages,' she whispered back.

'I'll watch.' Jamie giggled. 'He used to do that, didn't he?'

'A long time ago.' Claire smiled at the memory. Nowadays, with a heavy research load as well as his on-call duties, Ben rarely had time, but when Jamie had been much younger he'd read to him most evenings. 'And only to see if you were paying attention.'

She went into the living-room and flicked through some general practice journals which had arrived that day, not seeing the words, just filling in time before Ben came back. A while later her bleeper went off, and she leaned across for the phone. It was one of her own patients, worried that she'd forgotten to take her blood pressure tablet that morning.

'I feel fine but should I take one now?' she asked.

'Only then there'll be another one first thing in the morning.'

'It doesn't matter that you've skipped just one,' Claire said soothingly. 'That particular tablet lasts a long time in the bloodstream so you don't have to worry. Take your next dose as normal.'

'Oh, thank you, Doctor.' Her patient sounded relieved, and Claire smiled slightly. 'I was so worried. Sorry to disturb you.'

'That's all right, Mrs Skittrall. Sleep well.'

Almost immediately after she'd put the phone down her bleeper shrilled again. This time it was one of Warren's patients, a man who told her he'd had flu and had taken a week off work. Now he demanded a sickness certificate to take to his employer in the morning.

Claire sighed, suspecting, from the tone of his request, that this was going to be difficult. 'How is your flu?'

'Nothing wrong with me now,' he told her flatly. 'All I want is my certificate.'

'You'll have to come to the surgery tomorrow,' she told him. 'There'll be someone there from eight o'clock.'

'I start work at seven.'

'Perhaps you could come in during your lunch-break?'

'This isn't on.' He sounded belligerent now. 'You're supposed to do house calls twenty-four hours. It's my taxes and my national insurance that pay you. Why can't you come now?'

'The out-of-hours service is for emergencies,' Claire said, keeping her voice calm. 'Mr Donaldson, if you want a certificate you will have to come in tomorrow—' But then she stopped, rolling her eyes at the dialling tone. He'd hung up on her.

When she lowered the receiver Ben was there, leaning against the doorframe watching her, his dark eyes shadowed. 'Problems?'

'Someone else wanting routine work out of hours.' She lifted one shoulder wearily. 'I don't think they understand that the doctors they see during the days are the same ones who work the nights as well.'

'So turn the after-hours work over to an agency,' he said meaningfully. 'Or use locums. Most of the other practices are doing it and it would take some of the pressure off.'

'We prefer our own methods,' she said stiffly. It wasn't the first time he'd suggested such a thing and she resented the implication that she couldn't cope. 'And I wasn't complaining, merely making conversation. I believe we should offer our patients the best service we can.'

'Is that what they get?' He sounded sceptical. 'Do tired, overworked general practitioners really give the best possible service?'

'We know all the patients,' she said abruptly. 'They get excellent treatment with good communication between all the doctors involved. Yes, I think they get the best possible service.'

'You're always so defensive about this.'

'Because you're always attacking,' she countered. 'You don't understand...' But then, remembering that she'd vowed to make more of an effort to improve things between them, she swallowed the words. She took a deep breath, registering that he still waited. 'Er, did you...have a good day?' she asked jerkily.

His eyes narrowed. 'What?'

'Today. You must have finished early. Did you have a good day?'

Ben frowned at her. 'A normal day,' he said finally. He levered himself away from the doorframe. 'Coffee?'

'Please.' Smoothing her slightly dampened palms against the fabric of her jeans, she followed him into the kitchen. 'Ben, about what you said last night,' she said quickly, hurrying to get it over with. 'About another baby. I don't think...I mean I think we should wait.'

'Wait?' He'd put the kettle on to boil and now he folded his arms and looked at her. 'How long?'

'Six months,' she said quickly. Six months would give them time to work things out, if things could be worked out. And, if they couldn't, six months was enough time in which to decide their alternatives. If he was looking for a quick solution to their problems, having a baby wasn't it—and getting pregnant without knowing for sure that their relationship was going to survive wouldn't be fair to either of them.

'We both need time to consider this,' she continued. 'It's a huge step and would mean a lot of changes.' Seeing the tightness of his mouth, she changed tack. 'I'm not saying I don't want one, but I think we should see how...how we both feel about it in six months.'

'In the meantime, you're determined to continue working.'

'Of course.' She jerked. 'This isn't just to stop me from working, is it?' she demanded sharply. 'Because if that's the only reason—'

'It's not.' He lifted his palm as if to stop her talking. 'And last night you admitted you wanted one, too.'

'That doesn't mean it's something we should rush into,' she said huskily, wondering what game he was playing now by pretending to ignore their difficulties. Even if she was wrong about Lisa, and right then she doubted she'd ever have the courage to bring the subject up, their problems were myriad. First and foremost, the fact that they argued almost every time they spoke. 'There's no hurry, is there?'

Ben's mouth compressed and he turned away from her to pour the now boiling water on top of the ground coffee. 'Because your work is more important?'

'It isn't that,' she insisted. 'Six months.' Her tone was imploring now. 'It's not a long time. Till November. Then we'll decide.'

His gaze lowered to her breasts which, to her dismay,

promptly tightened under his scrutiny, then his eyes dropped to her stomach and he studied her with a thoughtfulness that made her begin to ache.

'That means a baby in August. You'll be heavily pregnant over summer. You'll be hot,' he said softly, his eyes lifting to her breasts again. 'Uncomfortable.'

'It might take longer than that before I conceive,' she mumbled nervously, crossing her arms to conceal the sudden arousal she knew he must have noticed. He was playing with her, of course, she knew that. Toying with her. Experience had taught him that he didn't need to touch her to arouse her, but her involuntary response now struck her as ironic, considering that last night she'd fled from him when they'd discussed this same issue. 'Months,' she added thickly. 'It might take months to get pregnant. Perhaps a year or more.'

His gaze rose to her mouth and made her shiver. 'It didn't with Jamie.'

'No.' Her blood thudded in her thighs and she shifted uneasily beneath the provocation of his regard. 'Well, I'm older now.'

'Not so much older.'

His eyes were very dark and she felt her breath come faster. 'We'll see.'

'We will.'

She barely heard him for the sound of her pulse, loud in her ears. She knew exactly what was happening to her, understood that his arousal of her was deliberate, but after so long she didn't know what to do. 'Ben…?'

But he didn't move. 'Yes, Claire?'

'Please…?' But she hesitated, rose onto her toes then down again, unsure. She was used to him taking control and now, because he didn't, he left her confused. If this was revenge for her turning him down yesterday then her nervousness now must be giving him satisfaction, she realised faintly.

But there was no satisfaction in his expression, only

an intensity that was as guarded as it was watchful, and he made no move to touch her.

'Coffee must be ready,' she said abruptly, twisting herself free of his gaze and spinning to the cupboards so she could fetch some mugs.

To her relief, Ben's attention swung to the drink and he pushed down on the plunger to filter the coffee, allowing her one brief unobserved moment to collect her thoughts and try and calm herself.

He loaded the things onto a tray and carried it through into the living-room, watching enigmatically as she switched on another lamp and took the armchair further from the table against the far wall.

He poured them each a drink, brought her hers, then relaxed onto the couch, his long legs stretched in front of him. 'Wendy rang tonight,' he said coolly. 'Her mother's still unwell. She asked for another week off.'

Claire leaned back in her chair and closed her eyes. 'What did you say?'

'I didn't have much choice. I should manage to get away early enough to get Jamie from school next Tuesday—and I should finish at least by six on Wednesday,' he added, surprising her into blinking at him.

He didn't normally volunteer to come home early. Usually she had to ask long in advance.

'Which nights are you on call?'

'After the weekend, just Wednesday,' she said huskily. 'I'll ask Mary if she'd mind looking after Jamie after school for a couple of days and see if Mum can cover another two. If you can get there Tuesday that'll cover the week.'

Mary, their neighbour, to whom Jamie had gone that afternoon, had three young children—including two boys at school with Jamie—so it wasn't inconvenient to fetch him at the same time. Kind, but already frazzled from looking after her own boisterous children, she refused to take any money for minding Jamie, and as

Claire could so rarely return the favour she was careful not to take advantage of her.

Claire lifted her coffee. 'Are you still very busy?' she asked carefully, still self-conscious and hating the awkwardness that made her nervous about speaking with him and hoping that she didn't sound as stilted to him as she did to herself. 'Are your colleagues still away?'

'Until next week,' he confirmed.

'And are the wards full? How's your clinic list these days?'

His gaze swung to her. 'Come on, Claire. Are you telling me you're actually interested?'

She tensed, resenting that. She'd always taken an interest, even if it suited him to pretend otherwise. Once, before Ben and then her subsequent pregnancy with Jamie, she'd considered a career in surgery and she still found the field fascinating. 'I'm interested in everything you do.'

'Really?' His raised brow suggested he had doubts. 'You surprise me.'

'What?' She heard herself becoming defensive now. 'Why?'

'Because it's been months since you've shown this interest you now protest so emphatically.'

Her fists clenched. Frightened that they were risking descending into another argument, she knew that she had to stop this now. She bit at her lower lip, her nervousness increasing but knowing that if they were to work through this she had no choice but to confront him. 'I don't want to argue any more,' she appealed. 'Please. I'm trying. Can't you at least meet me halfway?'

With a muttered curse he lowered his cup to the floor and stood, his hands sliding restlessly into the pockets of his jeans. He strode to the window, looked out onto the darkened street and then swung back to face her, his expression brooding. 'What does that mean?'

Unable to sustain his regard, she lowered her head and

focused on the depths of her coffee. 'Stop pretending you don't understand.'

'Perhaps I don't.'

'It obviously suits you to say you don't.'

'You're talking in riddles.'

'I'm not the only one.' She raised her head then, her pain masked. 'You know things have been difficult lately,' she said rawly. 'We barely speak—when we do it's mostly to fight. You're hardly ever here. And you haven't…we haven't…slept together for so long—'

'That bothers you?'

'Of course it bothers me!' Despite her determination to hide her emotions, her voice was choked. His rejection in the kitchen could not have been plainer and it still hurt.

His expression was unreadable. 'Last night—'

'Last night was different,' she cried. 'I was…shocked. Upset. Ben, it's been almost a year—'

'You've never said you minded.'

'What exactly was I supposed to say?' Unable to stay still she surged from her chair and paced the floor, refusing to look at him.

'You could try asking me.'

She should have, she *might* have, before, but not now—not with her suspicions about Lisa. Not when she couldn't bear to hear him tell her why not—why he couldn't touch her, why he no longer had any interest in her.

'I—I'm not asking you to touch me now,' she said faintly, protecting her pride although she still ached from her earlier arousal. 'That's not what I want.' Only tonight that wasn't true. 'I just want us to get along.'

But it seemed that her simple plea enraged him because he swore. Violently. 'Get along?' he grated. 'Get along? What the hell does that mean?'

'Stop arguing.' She turned to stare at the elegant Venetian gold clock on the mantelpiece, a wedding present from his parents. 'Spend time with each other, with Jamie, as a family. Is that so much to ask?'

'God, Claire! Have you any idea—?'

But whatever else he was going to say was interrupted by the high-pitched squeal of her bleeper, and he broke off abruptly.

Shaking, Claire reached blindly for the telephone. It was one of Warren's patients, a young mother, worried about her five-year-old. 'She's got a temperature and a headache,' she told Claire. 'I was concerned...there's been so much in the papers lately...Could it be this meningitis?'

'Unlikely,' Claire told her, when she'd described her symptoms which included a sore throat and runny nose. 'More likely to be just a cold. But I'll come and see her straight away.'

When she'd finished her conversation she darted a quick look at Ben under her lashes as she moved towards the door. 'I have to go,' she said huskily. 'Sorry.'

His expression suggested that he doubted it, and privately she acknowledged that he was probably right to question the sincerity of her apology. 'I'll wait up.'

'No, don't.' She met his gaze bravely as she shoved her feet into the trainers she kept by the door, then stooped to collect her bag. 'It's late and I could get another call.' She opened the door, holding on to the edge of it. 'But we do need to talk. Properly. Not tonight. After Scotland. After the weekend.'

His face was shadowed and, from where she stood, grim. 'All right.'

Suddenly and unaccountably finding herself on the verge of tears, she slipped out the door and pulled it shut behind her.

The child had a viral respiratory-tract infection, Claire decided, after examining her thoroughly. She had a mild headache but there was no neck stiffness or rash, and she didn't object when Claire shone a torch directly into her eyes. 'It's not meningitis,' she explained to the worried parents. 'Relax. A day or two off school if she's still unwell, lots of fluids, paracetamol now and another dose in four hours if her temperature is still up.'

The other woman nodded. 'Does she need any antibiotics?'

'It'll be a virus,' Claire told her. 'Antibiotics won't help and using them just encourages resistance to develop. Her ears are fine and so is her throat and her tonsils aren't inflamed.'

'Thank you.' Both parents accompanied her to her car. 'Sorry,' the child's mother said as Claire opened her door, 'about it being so late, Doctor. We didn't mean to waste your time.'

'You haven't.' Claire smiled her reassurance, understanding the concerns of young children's parents. She'd worried herself about such things when Jamie had been smaller and still had difficulty regarding her own son with a doctor's objectivity. 'It's important to rule out meningitis,' she said firmly, 'but I'm happy to come out anyway. Call me again if you're worried about anything else.'

The light was on in Ben's bedroom when she arrived home and although the door was ajar, after kissing Jamie who was soundly asleep, she went directly to her own room.

She saw Ben only briefly on Friday morning. In a hurry to get to work, after being called out at five in the morning to see an elderly man breathless from heart failure whom she'd had to admit to hospital, she only had time for a quick shower and change of clothes, before taking Jamie to school and rushing to the surgery.

'Claire…?' David, whose office was next to hers in the surgery, put his head around the door as she arrived and blew her a clumsy kiss. 'Just wanted to thank you for Angus Donaldson this morning.'

'Angus Donaldson?' She sent him a blank look, then

frowned, wondering at the bloodshot bleariness of his pale eyes. 'Sorry...? Oh,' she remembered, 'the man who wanted the sick note?'

David grimaced. 'He was here at eight o'clock when I arrived. Furious face the colour of a plum. I thought he was going to knock my block off.'

Although it wasn't really funny, David looked so fed up that she laughed. 'Sorry. He wanted me to come out last night and I refused. Was he genuine?'

'Hardly. I gave him the usual spiel about not issuing notes unless he comes to us when he's actually ill but you'll understand I didn't actually argue the point.'

'I get the picture.' She tilted her head. 'David, are you all right? You're pale. Have you got a headache?'

'Eyestrain,' he said abruptly. 'Warren's been on at me again. I'm behind on my paperwork and I've been working late at home to try and catch up.'

'You don't look well.'

'You can talk.' His gaze narrowed on his face. 'You haven't exactly been a bundle of smiles lately. Problems at home?'

'I'm fine,' she protested. 'Just a little tired.'

'Just as well. Being strained and emotional is supposed to be my role.' His mouth turned down deprecatingly. 'Nothing I can do?'

'Nothing.' But her smile thanked him for caring. Of her three partners, she was closest to David and, considering what he'd been through with Rebecca, she knew he might have valuable advice to offer. But, then, however difficult things became, she also knew she'd never be able to confide in him the way he had in her. Her marriage was too private to ever discuss. 'Thanks for offering, though, David. I appreciate it.'

'How about dinner?' he ventured. 'Tonight. Or tomorrow, if it suits better and you're not too busy on call. Away from here so you can feel more free to talk. Tell Ben you're working—he won't know.'

'Ben's away this weekend,' she said, puzzled that he thought she was capable of that sort of dishonesty and puzzled, too, that he thought there would be a need for her to make excuses if she wanted to spend time with him. During the time surrounding his marriage break-up they had met several times outside work when he'd needed someone to talk to. But not lately, at least not in the last six months or so. And now, while the thought of having to smile and chat socially as if nothing was wrong didn't appeal to her in the slightest, she didn't want to hurt him by explaining that she'd never feel free to confide in him as he seemed to think she should.

'The child-minder's away too so it's just me and Jamie,' she added. 'I'm looking forward to spending some time with him. I don't want to go out.'

'Bring Jamie, too,' he said. 'Ben's away the whole weekend?'

'Doing fellowship teaching in Edinburgh.' She made a mock grimace as she flicked through some laboratory results which had been left on her desk for her to check. 'Hard work, by the sounds of it.'

She glanced up then and saw that David's eyebrows had risen. 'He's going alone?'

'Perhaps some of his colleagues are going, too—I'm not sure.' She kept her expression calm although inwardly she tensed, wondering if David's probing meant he knew more than he'd let on. He'd said he'd seen Lisa and Ben together at a restaurant but perhaps he'd seen something more? Perhaps they'd been kissing or holding hands? Her heart thumped coldly and her fists clenched around the results she was clutching. Perhaps he was wondering whether to warn her?

'Ben's away a lot, isn't he?' His tone sharper now, David continued, 'Even when he's not away he seems to be on call most nights. Doesn't sound like you even see each other that often.'

'Often enough,' she said faintly. Deliberately she lowered her head, feigning an interest in some folders on her desk and hoping he'd realise that she didn't want him to tell her anything more. 'Thanks for the dinner invitation, David, but I really want some time with Jamie. Some other time, perhaps?'

'Fine.' She felt rather than saw him withdraw. 'But you know where I am if you change your mind.'

She managed a quick smile. 'Thank you.'

She'd assumed that Ben would be leaving for Scotland directly from work but in the early evening, when she arrived home after picking up Jamie from her mother's house, his Saab pulled up almost immediately behind her.

Then she saw Lisa, supremely groomed and poised as always, in the passenger seat beside him, and her careful smile of welcome froze on her face.

Through vision that seemed suddenly hazy, she watched the younger woman ease herself elegantly from the car, her smile, as she looked at Claire, little short of gloating.

CHAPTER FOUR

BEN, though, seemed either oblivious or determined to ignore the shock Claire knew she hadn't been able to conceal.

Apparently in a hurry, he swung his briefcase out of the boot of his car then paused briefly to kiss her cheek and greet Jamie, before directing his registrar ahead of them to the door.

'Make Lisa a coffee, will you, Claire?' he said briskly. 'While I pack. We're supposed to be at Heathrow in an hour and traffic's already bad.'

Claire astonished herself by being able to follow them into the house.

Jamie, though, she noted, had no reservations, and she was left fighting surging betrayal as he took the other woman's hand in his and tugged her towards the kitchen, chatting happily all the while, as if the pair of them were great friends.

Ignoring Ben's command about the coffee, Claire went directly to her room and sat on the edge of her bed, numb, wondering what this meant. That he was taking Lisa to Scotland with him for the weekend was awful enough, and something she'd rather not have known, but why had he brought her here? Was this an overt declaration of his feelings for Lisa? Why, then, was he so insistent about her having another child? Was this visit aimed at Lisa, aimed at showing her his family life so she wouldn't get ideas of taking him away from it?

Heaving herself from the bed she went to his room, standing in the door a few seconds, watching him pack, as she tried to think of what to say. 'I thought you'd be taking the train.'

He looked up quickly, the faint surprise she saw—perhaps that she'd ventured into the room they'd shared for so many years—quickly masked. 'We decided to fly,' he said flatly. 'We're picking up a hire car from the airport in Edinburgh.'

We. Claire felt sick. A hire car. So they could tour the sights, presumably. Clearly the teaching sessions, which had been the excuse for the weekend away, wouldn't be taking up every hour.

'I didn't...I didn't realise Lisa would be going with you,' she said finally.

'She usually does.' He went into the bathroom and returned with his sponge bag which he put into the case, before snapping the locks closed. 'I thought you realised.'

'No.' Claire pressed her back against the wall as he collected the case, then swivelled to claim a long raincoat from the wardrobe. There were a lot of things she hadn't realised until recently. 'I didn't know.'

'She helps out generally and this year she's doing some tutoring herself.' He came towards her. 'I didn't mean to bring her here,' he said, his voice lower now as if he realised how shaken she was. 'I'm sorry if you're upset but we were late getting away from work. She already had her bags. It seemed the easiest thing to do.'

Easiest for whom? she wanted to shriek, but of course she didn't. 'I didn't make coffee.'

'No.' Close to her now, he bent slightly as if to kiss her cheek again, but she jerked away. 'I shouldn't have asked,' he said deeply. One finger stroked the softness of her averted cheek. 'Claire, you're overreacting.'

She clenched her fists, knowing that this was her opportunity, and at that moment, for the first time, it seemed worse not to know. 'You're having an affair with her.'

'Is that what you think?'

His question was quiet, thoughtful almost, and her head came up sharply. 'Aren't you?'

'Are you asking me?'

'Have you slept with her?'

'No.'

She recoiled. The answer she'd longed for, the answer that should have given her pleasure, relief, did none of that. He hadn't said, 'of course not.' He hadn't told her that was ridiculous. He hadn't told her that he couldn't sleep with another woman while he was in love with her, his wife. Just 'no'.

It wasn't enough. There'd been no hesitation. He hadn't sounded surprised and she understood immediately that he'd been expecting her accusation, had anticipated that question. There were things he wasn't telling her, many things.

She held herself still. 'Are you going to sleep with her this weekend?'

He didn't say anything but something, quickly concealed in his eyes, made pain stab through her like a kitchen knife. Ben didn't lie, she acknowledged. Never. Not even the small social lies that could make life easier. He wouldn't deny something if he felt he couldn't.

'You'd better go,' she said dully, wanting him to go now, wanting him to leave. Immediately. Before she did something, said something, she'd be ashamed of.

But for once she saw him uncertain. 'We can't talk about this now,' he said harshly, his face dark, flushed, as if this was affecting him as much as it was her. 'There's no time and it's too important.'

'Leave.' She lowered her head, held her breath. 'Please.'

'Claire...?'

'Please, Ben.' She surged away, backed against the other wall, squeezed her stinging eyes shut, and turned to face the wall so that the toes of her shoes scraped the stained wood of the skirting-board. Glad that she was numb now because otherwise the pain would have been unbearable, she heard nothing at first—silence—but then she heard him move, and there were sounds of them leaving, Jamie's cheerful farewells, the slamming of the boot and finally the sound of Ben's car.

By the time Jamie came upstairs to find her she'd rearranged her features into a semblance of ordinariness. She hugged him, then held him tightly until his faintly self-conscious wriggles made her release him.

'Let's get McDonald's,' she said brightly—perhaps too brightly she registered faintly, but wanting to distract him before he said anything in case it was to mention the other woman's name. She appreciated his whoop of delight at the unexpected treat. 'And a video. And if you're not too tired you can stay up late and watch it all, I promise. OK, darling?'

'OK.' He tugged her towards the stairs as if worried she'd change her mind. 'Come on, Mummy. Let's go.'

She was on call from the next morning. Her mother came just before nine and Claire made an effort to muster a smile and to converse normally over breakfast, determined not to let her guess there was any problem.

Besides, her mother was Ben's greatest fan, she reflected with a bitterness that seemed to have become part of her state of mind lately. If she knew there were problems in the marriage she'd blame Claire, not her golden boy.

Thankfully, the weekend was busy. There was a Saturday morning clinic at the surgery, run by whoever had been on call Friday night—Warren, this time—but as soon as that finished the calls started coming to her. She arrived home around midnight on Saturday night to find a note from her mother, telling her that Ben had called with a number where she could reach him. For a long time she just sat and stared at the number, then finally she screwed it up and threw it into the bin.

On Sunday she went into the surgery and spent a few relatively quiet hours in the morning, catching up with paperwork, then the afternoon and evening were busy again.

Astonishingly, what hadn't changed, she realised as she drove to another call late that night, was that if Ben was willing she still wanted to preserve their marriage. For Jamie's sake, she told herself, she wanted them to stay together. And while the thought of Lisa hurt, hurt terribly, Claire couldn't say she hadn't suspected already. These things happened, she told herself, trying to look at the issue pragmatically—her experience and training in marriage guidance giving her that much knowledge at least. Marriages survived affairs, sometimes even strengthened.

But it wasn't going to be easy.

She arrived home after midnight and he was waiting for her. Surprised, because she hadn't expected him back until the following day, she started when he opened the door before she'd even had time to get out her key.

Avoiding his probing gaze, she concentrated only on getting away from him. 'Not now, Ben,' she said dully. She was physically as well as emotionally exhausted and, despite her determination to fight for him, her control was thin and this was too important to risk damaging with an outburst. 'Please. It's been a horrendous weekend and I haven't had enough sleep. I don't have the energy for you. Let me go to bed.'

Mutely he stepped back but not far enough for her to get past him without brushing against him, and when she did she recoiled, shocked that even knowing it must only be hours since he'd been with Lisa the touch of his arm against her hip still had the power to rouse her.

'Avoiding this won't help,' he said quietly, as she stumbled up the stairs.

'You'd be surprised.' She didn't stop.

They had breakfast together next morning but her mother was still there and Jamie, of course, and apart from a brief but loaded exchange of looks when they greeted each other there was no opportunity to talk.

Her mother questioned Ben about his weekend but his clipped responses soon discouraged her and she meandered into generalities. 'You both work too hard,' she scolded. 'Poor Claire's hardly been home at all since Saturday morning. And you off...doing that teaching thing. It's been years since the pair of you had a holiday together. When are you going to get away somewhere?'

'I can't take any time,' Claire said crisply, finishing her cereal. 'We're too busy now. Warren's away for a month over summer in the school holidays so they can't spare me as well.'

'Even a weekend.' Her mother helped Jamie spread butter on his toast. 'I could look after Jamie for a weekend. You could go to Eastbourne. Or Torquay. One of the women I play golf with has just come back and she says it's lovely there at the moment.'

'We very rarely get a weekend free at the same time,' Claire countered quickly, not looking at Ben although she sensed his watchfulness. 'But thanks for offering.' She checked her watch, gulped the rest of her coffee and kissed her mother's forehead as she stood to collect her things. 'And thanks for taking Jamie to school.' She kissed her son, nodded somewhere vaguely in the direction of her silent husband and fled.

On Saturday she'd been too busy to get to the hospital so in the break between her Monday morning calls and her afternoon clinic Claire went up to see Rachel, her little patient with leukaemia.

The SHO looking after her told her it was too soon to see a dramatic drop in Rachel's white blood cell count after the chemotherapy but, since she was still being nursed in a side room, Claire washed her hands and

donned one of the plastic aprons hanging outside her
room just as a precaution.

Rachel seemed cheerful and she proudly showed her
through a huge bundle of cards which her school class-
mates had made for her. 'Mummy's gone to lunch,' she
told her. 'She's going to bring me back something
yummy.'

'Lucky you.' Claire smiled at her excitement. 'You're
not sick, then?'

'Not too much. The doctors told me I was going to
be yesterday, but I wasn't.'

'Not too many needles?'

'They gave me this.' She lifted her pyjama top to reveal a length of white tubing that stuck out of a broad
dressing across the right side of her thin little chest.
Called a Hickman line, Claire knew that the tube was
inserted directly into a large central vein and could be
used for taking blood samples as well as for administer-
ing fluids and chemotherapy, diminishing the need for
other needles. 'It stays there all the time,' Rachel told
her.

'Until you're better,' Claire said. She stayed for half
an hour but when Julie still hadn't returned by one
o'clock she had to say her goodbyes and leave or else
risk being late for her afternoon clinic.

When she arrived at the surgery the receptionist
handed her a message from the registrar working for the
psychiatrist who was looking after her patient, Susan
Drury. It said that Susan had been discharged that morning and gave the address and telephone number of the
halfway house where she was staying. Claire took the
note into her office, deciding to give Susan a few days
to settle in before she called her.

One of her patients that afternoon had recently been
under Ben's care at the hospital. An otherwise reasonably well, sixty-five-year-old woman, Claire had referred
her to him for treatment of claudication, or pain on ex-

ercise, in her right leg. Ben had told her the details of the patient's treatment but Claire skimmed the letter his house officer had sent her on Mrs Wilson's discharge to make sure she hadn't missed anything.

According to the note, Ben had investigated the pain with an arteriogram, a test involving injecting dye into the major blood vessel supplying the leg and taking a series of X-rays, and in Mrs Wilson's case the films had shown a significant narrowing in the femoral artery, caused by atherosclerosis. Ben had gone on to operate and bypass the narrowing with a graft, which had restored the blood supply to the leg.

Today she'd come to have her stitches removed. 'Mr Howard was very good,' Mrs Wilson gushed, perching with renewed agility on the edge of the examination table so Claire could inspect the narrow wound that stretched along her thigh. 'He takes so much time over his patients,' she continued. 'We never felt rushed. He's very popular.'

'I'm glad things went well.'

'And so handsome.' Mischievous green eyes twinkled at her, telling Claire that she was well aware of who Ben was. 'None of us could keep our eyes off him.'

'I don't think he even notices any more.' Claire smiled quickly at her.

'Probably takes it for granted,' her patient said lightly. 'It must get like that eventually. Does your son take after his father?'

'Same eyes but fairer hair. My mother thinks he's the image of Ben.'

'A few more years and he'll have the girls chasing after him.'

'He's more interested in his swimming at the moment,' Claire said. 'Thank goodness.' She smiled again, pleased with the look and feel of Mrs Wilson's leg. Prior to the surgery it had been rather cool and mottled, in keeping with the reduced blood supply, but now it was warm and close to a normal colour. 'You've done very well.'

'He wants to see me again in November,' Mrs Wilson informed her. 'He thinks I might need an operation on the other side next year.'

'Did he tell you anything else?'

'I've stopped smoking,' her patient said sheepishly. 'Forty-two days now, that's six weeks since the last. You were right—he was very strict about that.'

'Well done.' Claire nodded her approval. She'd been trying to convince her patient to stop for years but clearly Ben had an authority that in Mrs Wilson's eyes she lacked. 'Nicotine patches?'

'He gave me some for the first month but now I seem to be getting along without them.'

'That's good news.' Claire stepped over to the sink and washed her hands. 'The wound looks excellent. Rest there for a few minutes while I ask one of the nurses to come and take the stitches out for you.'

She was in the kitchen around eight that evening washing the dishes from dinner, when she heard Ben's car outside. She knew that he was on call and guessed that his bleeper had sounded while he was driving home because she heard him open the front door and go straight to the telephone in the living-room.

She tensed, waiting, but when he came to the door his face, as he kissed Jamie, was preoccupied and she knew what he was going to say. 'I have to go back,' he said quickly, confirming her thoughts. 'There's been a pile-up. Six hurt. I'm needed in Theatre.'

'Take some fruit.' She hurried to the bowl and collected bananas and an apple for him. If he stayed late at the hospital he usually ate there, but when he came home early, like this, it normally signalled he hadn't had dinner. 'Shall I make sandwiches?'

'No time.' He checked his watch as he took the fruit. 'Thanks. I am hungry.'

Jamie was used to him making rushed appearances like this—used to both of them doing it—but he still came with her to the door to see him off. 'I had another swimming lesson today,' he told Ben.

'Well done.' Ben ruffled Jamie's head. 'Secret agents have to be good swimmers,' he said as he swung himself into his Saab. 'See you tomorrow, 007.'

'Bye.' Jamie waved.

Ben's eyes met hers for a brief, probing second, before he shut the door and accelerated out onto the street.

'Daddy's very important,' Jamie told her.

'I know, darling.' She smiled faintly at the pride in his voice.

'He's coming to my school tomorrow.'

'As long as there's no emergency at the hospital,' Claire said carefully. She shut the front door on the cool evening, hoping that Ben wouldn't have to disappoint him. Despite Ben's best intentions, it wouldn't be the first time it had happened. 'You know if there's an emergency he might have to stay at work.'

'He told me.' But he didn't seem concerned, instead asking with a casualness that she knew was entirely feigned, 'Want to play soldiers, Mummy?'

'No.' She laughed, then tickled him until he squealed. 'Rascal. You know I don't know the faintest thing about soldiers and you always cheat. Chinese checkers,' she announced, 'or nothing. Best of three, then straight to bed so Mummy can do some work. OK?'

'OK.' He ran to get the board. 'I'm not as good as I used to be. Nana won all the time on Sunday.'

'I'm kinder than Nana,' she told him crisply. 'Besides, I've seen her cheating more than you.'

The next day there was no phone call from Ben's secretary to warn that he wouldn't be able to get Jamie, and when Claire arrived home just after six Ben was playing some kind of football on the back lawn with

Jamie and Mary's three children from next door plus two of the younger children from the other side.

The goals were marked by picnic chairs which Ben must have retrieved from the garage rafters. There were shrieks and yells and someone had given Jamie a whistle and she saw he was taking his role seriously, blowing fiercely whenever anyone moved as well as diving vigorously for the ball himself.

Laughingly fending off a tackle from one of the youngest of the tribe, Ben waved at her. 'Help,' he called. 'We're a man down. We need a goalie.'

'You need a coach,' she countered. 'Look at your attack—it's appalling.'

'Ha. Ha.' But he grinned at her, a broad, unguarded grin that made her breath catch. 'You're all mouth.'

'Let me get changed.' She felt lighter suddenly, happier. Tonight her briefcase full of paperwork could wait, she decided. 'I'll show you,' she warned, turning to go back inside.

It only took her a few minutes to pull on jeans and a sweater and trainers, and Jamie blew his whistle at her when she reappeared on the lawn. 'Mummy's on my side,' he declared breathlessly.

'Darling, you're the ref,' she told him, scooping up the ball which had been temporarily abandoned and tucking it under her arm. Then she stopped, wondering if she should have done that. 'Is this football or rugby?'

'Football,' they all chorused, but that didn't stop four of the children tackling her.

When she finally disentangled herself, flushed and dishevelled and ball-less, Ben jogged with the others to the chairs where Jamie kicked a goal. 'I think our attack's OK,' Ben taunted, patting her denim-covered rear as he ran back.

'I thought we were on the same side,' she protested, tingling from his touch.

'What side?' He laughed, ran backwards and caught

the ball one of the others had kicked high. 'It's each man for himself.'

'And each woman,' she cried, running and catching him by surprise with a well-placed leg into his shin which made him stumble and release the ball. Claire snatched it up, threw it to the boy who stood nearest the opposite goal, then cheered as he flung it between the chairs.

'Consider that your last.' Ben laughed, his hand lingering slightly on her back on his way down the lawn again. 'I know your tactics now.'

'Victory at any price,' she told him minutes later as she pushed him to the ground and scored the next goal, ignoring Jamie's frantic whistles of protest and laughing as one of Mary's sons picked up the ball and ran it directly through the goal again for another score.

'Mummy, you're cheating,' Jamie shouted, sounding pleased.

'Not as badly as Daddy, darling,' she told him. She also knew that in the spirit of the game Ben had allowed her to fell him—if he'd wanted to resist, her puny weight would never have budged him.

They played for another hour or so, a happy, easy, laughing hour, and then Mary called for her boys and the children from the other side drifted away too, and Claire took Jamie upstairs and ran him a bath.

'Wash that hair,' she told him firmly, leaving him with the shampoo. 'It's full of grass.'

Outside, Ben was brushing off his trainers. 'Jamie had beans earlier,' he told her, when she walked into the kitchen. 'I was going to grill a steak for myself. Want one?'

'I'll do it.' She smiled as she opened the refrigerator, light-hearted and hopeful after the easy camaraderie of the football. 'I'll cook. You do the bedtime story. Has he done his homework?'

'As soon as he got home.' He came inside. 'I spoke

to his teacher this afternoon. He must have told her I was coming because she came out to meet me. Jamie's grades have slipped these last two terms.'

Claire turned around, sobering abruptly. 'Much?'

'She's worried.' He was watching her, frowning slightly. 'She asked if there were any problems at home.'

Claire swallowed. 'What did you say?'

'Not a lot.'

'What are we going to do?'

'I don't know.' He sat at the breakfast bar, folded his arms. 'Does he seem unhappy to you?'

'No. At least not overtly so. Last week when he over-heard us arguing about your dinner at the college he asked about it,' she said faintly. 'But, apart from that…well, he seems like a well-adjusted child.'

'We're hardly impartial observers,' Ben said softly. 'And his teacher did make a special effort to talk to me.'

'Yes. Well.' Claire didn't know what else to say. Her good humour had evaporated.

Mechanically she selected the paper-wrapped parcel that contained the steaks, shut the refrigerator door and took the parcel to the bench. The thought that the problems in their relationship might be damaging their son's progress made her feel sick, but she was already trying her best to mend that relationship. She went back to the fridge and assembled the ingredients for a salad. 'What do you suggest we do?'

'You could start by looking at me.'

She lifted her head and met his dark regard without flinching. 'Does that help?'

His face hardened. 'Claire, about Scotland—'

'I don't want to know,' she said sharply, on an intake of breath. 'Not anything.'

'Still—'

'I don't want to talk about it.' She tore her gaze away, picked up the knife and sliced viciously into a tomato. Whether he'd technically had sex with Lisa or not made little difference, and she definitely didn't want it confirmed if he had. She didn't even want to think about it. Ignorance was hardly bliss, she acknowledged, but it seemed less risky than the alternative. The only thing that really mattered, she decided, was what happened now. 'Just tell me if you're leaving.'

He let her chop three tomatoes into virtual pulp before he spoke. 'I'm not going anywhere.'

Her shoulders sagged but she refused to look at him. She scooped the tomato flesh into a wooden bowl, then reached for a cucumber. He was staying. That gave her time. Everything else she could work on. Tonight—the football game—they'd all had fun together. It was a promising start.

'Is that what you wanted to hear?'

She nodded. Once she would have wanted to protect her pride, she acknowledged, but now she couldn't pretend about something so important. Lifting the board, she scraped ragged cucumber slices into the bowl. 'At least we both know where we stand,' she said heavily, still not looking at him as she moved to the sink to rinse the lettuce. 'We can get on with our lives.'

'And Jamie?'

'I'll try and give him extra help. When Wendy gets back I'll go with her to speak to his teacher. She might have ideas about how we can work with him after school.'

Still avoiding his gaze, she turned her attention to the torn lettuce leaves, dabbed them dry with a paper towel and dismally surveyed the ragged chaos that was her salad. 'Vinaigrette or mayonnaise?'

'Your choice.' As if irritated by the triviality of the question, Ben's tone hardened. Out of the corner of her eye she saw him ease himself off the stool. 'I'll check Jamie.'

She went to the stairs a while later and heard Ben reading to him so she returned to the kitchen and put the grill on to heat. When he returned the steaks were ready to serve.

Conversation over dinner was desultory but civil and neither of them mentioned anything about their earlier discussion. From time to time, though, she caught him looking at her—as if he was expecting something more from her, she thought, but she was at a loss to know exactly what and so said nothing.

Afterwards, after another one of those puzzling looks—almost impatient this time—he retreated to the study, claiming he had to work. She read for awhile, watched the news and then, when he still hadn't appeared by eleven, she went to bed.

Saturday, to Jamie's delight and her own mixed feelings—the most prominent of which seemed to be nervousness—Ben came with them to the Natural History Museum for the morning. Later they went to a hamburger restaurant in Chelsea for lunch.

The restaurant was filled with families that looked like theirs but, sitting back in her chair, Claire mused about how deceptive appearances could be. There hadn't been any arguments since their discussion on Tuesday night and superficially she and Ben were getting on better than they had in months. Jamie seemed thrilled about having them both together but there was no intimacy between them, no secret conversations or smiles, just occasional searching looks that she was no closer to deciphering than she had ever been.

She saw a couple at the next table exchange a smile over the heads of their children, the sort of smile she and Ben used to share, and her stomach contracted. Despite their truce, Ben still hadn't touched her. Did that mean that after being with Lisa he no longer found her attractive?

'Are you on call Monday?' Ben's quiet words drew her thoughts back to the present.

'Tuesday and Friday.' Using her napkin, she mopped

at the damp ring Jamie's cola had left on the table. 'Although I'll swap Tuesday with David's Wednesday so I can get to my teaching,' she added jerkily. 'Why?'

'Duncan Allbright's retirement,' he said, referring to one of his surgical colleagues at the hospital. 'He's having a small function—drinks, some food perhaps. I thought you might like to go.'

She stared at him. This was work-related so Lisa would surely be there. What was he saying? And, whatever he was saying, could she cope with coming face to face with the other woman? 'But we haven't heard from Wendy yet. What if she's not back?'

'I asked your mother,' he said coolly. 'She's happy to pick Jamie up from school. She can take him to her house for the night.'

'You asked...?' She stared at him, bewildered. 'You asked my mother?'

'Yes.'

'Oh, great.' Jamie looked pleased. 'I can play with Rex.'

Jamie loved Rex, her mother's spaniel, but he didn't often see the dog because when her mother looked after him she normally came to the house, and as Claire had a mild allergy to dogs Rex stayed at home, looked after by a neighbour.

'When did you ask her?' Claire said abruptly.

'I called her on Thursday.' Ben lifted a napkin and wiped some tomato sauce from the corner of Jamie's mouth.

'You didn't say anything to me.'

'I'm saying something now.' He looked directly at her. 'Well?'

'Please, Mummy.' Jamie was watching her, too. 'I haven't seen Rex in ages.'

That was an exaggeration, she realised absently. He'd spent the previous Friday afternoon at her mother's home. But she didn't say anything, wondering if Ben had deliberately chosen to wait until Jamie was with them to voice his invitation. With Jamie listening so avidly, and her determination not to let him sense conflict between them, she could hardly refuse his invitation. 'I suppose,' she said finally, her eyes meeting Ben's dark ones with a look she knew would tell him she recognised her hand had been forced. 'What time?'

'Six to six-thirty.' Now Ben had had his way, although his reasons for wanting her there mystified her, he turned back to his food.

On Sunday afternoon after Ben had barbecued sausages, which they ate sitting outside on the lawn, they went for a long walk to the river and along past where the annual Oxford and Cambridge boat race finished. They sat on a grassy bank and Jamie and Claire made daisy chains to go around their necks while Ben read one of the Sunday papers.

After a while Claire lay back on the grass, pulling her hat over her forehead to shade her eyes from the warm spring sunshine. 'Tomorrow,' she mused, lifting a lazy hand to shoo away a fly that buzzed across her, 'for this retirement thing. I...shall I come straight from work?'

'If that's easiest.' He didn't sound especially concerned one way or the other. She heard him turn a page of his paper.

'I'll come to your office, then. Around six.'

'Fine.'

'Fine.' She closed her eyes, wondering.

As they meandered slowly home, Jamie humming softly and trotting ahead of them, she slipped her hand into Ben's. He looked at her sharply, but instead of pulling away the warm hand curled around hers firmly and he slowed his stride slightly to match hers.

'Thank you,' she said quietly.

'For what?'

'This weekend.' She watched Jamie's head tilt back

as he followed a seagull's gliding progress across the river.

'Because of Jamie?'

'He's happy,' she prevaricated, avoiding a direct answer. They walked into a small cluster of midges and she tugged her hand free to wave them away, but when they were through he didn't take it back and she was too shy to initiate the contact again.

They both had work to do that evening and after Jamie went to bed she took her journals into the living-room while Ben went to the study where he could use the computer. But she found it hard to concentrate and after a while she went to find him. 'Busy?' she asked quietly.

'Nothing that can't wait.' He swivelled away from the screen and looked at her, his expression shadowed.

'I—I thought I'd go to bed,' she said, conscious that her fists had clenched tightly by her side and that her voice sounded husky. 'Are you tired?'

'Not especially.'

But he didn't move, didn't say anything else, and after a few tense waiting seconds she started to blush. Wordlessly she lowered her head and left him, her happiness in their weekend together spoiled.

Some of her despondency must have been obvious to her partners because she saw David watching her with concern on several occasions the next day during the children's clinic they shared. He came to see her as she was preparing to leave the surgery that evening, waiting while she nervously renewed her lipstick in preparation for Ben's colleague's retirement function.

'Whatever you say, Claire, it's obvious something's wrong,' he said, taking her bag and carrying it to her car for her.

'I'm fine.' She gave him a gentle smile as she opened the boot, standing back to let him load her bag into it. 'And thanks again for covering my duties tomorrow night. There's no other way I could get to my teaching.'

The corners of his mouth turned down. 'Swapping on-call nights is no big deal. After all, it's not as if I've got anything else to do.' He touched her shoulder, his regard intent. 'Claire, this is me, David. I know you. You don't have to pretend with me. What's wrong?'

'Goodness, obviously I look more haggard than usual.' She slammed the lid of the boot shut. 'I suppose I'm still tired.'

'It's more than that.' His hand shifted from her shoulder to her chin, and tilted her face towards him. 'And you look beautiful as always,' he murmured. 'Only worried. Is it Ben?'

'Of course not.' She backed away, embarrassed by his concern. 'Don't be silly. Ben's fine.'

'I didn't mean that.' She'd opened her door, but now his hand closed over hers on the handle and she saw that he was breathing fast. 'Claire, I hate seeing you like this. You shouldn't bottle everything up, it's unhealthy. You have to face your feelings—confront them. I want to help you.'

'David, I appreciate your concern—'

To her total astonishment he took her cheeks between his hands and pressed his mouth urgently to hers. When she didn't resist, standing there in stunned shock, his kiss warmed and his hands shifted to her back and lifted her against him.

'David...?' Coming to her senses, Claire pushed him away and twisted her head urgently to escape his mouth when it sought hers again. Stunned that she could ever have let it happen in the first place, she stared up at him, her eyes wide. His kiss had been warm and not unpleasant or frightening, but even at the risk of hurting him she definitely didn't want it repeated. 'What on earth are you doing?'

'I love you!' He looked anguished. 'I love you, Claire.'

She gasped, appalled. 'No!'

'Claire...?'

'No, you don't,' she said urgently. 'It's too soon. It's because of Rebecca, don't you see? Your feelings are still confused. You're making a horrible mistake.'

'We can make it work,' he said fiercely. 'Just give me a chance. Please. Ben's not right for you—he doesn't treat you the way you deserve to be treated. Can't you see that? He's obviously having an affair with that woman—'

'Stop it!' She shoved him away when he came towards her again. 'No, David. Don't say anything more.'

A door slammed close by and something about the suddenness of the noise made them both turn. Claire gasped, horrified. Ben was coming towards them, his expression grim. Her heart thundered. How much had he seen?

CHAPTER FIVE

'DAVID.'

'Ben.'

The two men greeted each other with a coldness that made Claire feel sick.

'I wasn't expecting you,' she told Ben quickly, registering the glitter in his eyes that told her he'd already realised that. 'I thought...I thought we were meeting at your office?'

'I decided to drive you to the hospital. That way one of us can have a drink.'

David's discomfort was practically palpable. 'Yes. Well, I'll leave you to it,' he blustered, backing away from Ben's icy stare. 'Goodnight, Claire. Have a good evening.' Before she could say anything he'd vanished back into the surgery.

She waited for the door to bang shut then turned to Ben, swallowing heavily. 'Your car or mine?'

'Mine.' He gripped her arm as they crossed the street, but although his face was set tight his grasp was not ungentle.

Muddled thoughts hurtled around inside her head during the drive to the hospital. Dimly she registered the traffic, Ben's smooth handling of the big car, parking outside and the walk to the seminar room in the department of surgery. It felt as if this was some sort of wild, horrible dream. David...the kiss...Ben.

The only reality, she acknowledged dazedly, was that her husband was furious. She could feel his anger like a dull throbbing heat surrounding her.

'Nothing happened,' she said faintly.

'You think I don't know that?' His voice was low, hard, grating, but his expression as he guided her into the already crowded room was carefully masked. 'We're only here because it would hurt Duncan if we weren't,' he said icily. 'Smile, say the right things and we'll be out of here in half an hour.'

But she didn't want to be alone with him again that quickly and as soon as she could, after greeting and congratulating Duncan Allbright—the surgeon who was retiring—and his wife—an anaesthetist she'd met several times before—she broke away. With Ben watching her closely, apart from fifteen minutes or so when she glimpsed him outside the room talking on a telephone in the foyer, Claire tried to ignore her self-consciousness and forced herself to play the gracious surgeon's wife. There was no sign of Lisa, which helped, and from other such functions she recognised many of the other staff members and through them met others.

Ben's SHO and his house officer introduced themselves to her. On six-month attachments, they'd been working for Ben since February, but until now she hadn't met either of them. They told her how much they enjoyed working with Ben.

'Hard work,' his house officer conceded. 'He demands total commitment but, then, that's part of what makes the job so satisfying. And he takes the time to teach while a lot of the surgeons don't these days, not properly.'

She smiled mechanically. 'Are you planning to continue in surgery?'

'I think so.' He shrugged. 'Haven't made up my mind. Also it's hard to get training positions at the moment, especially here.'

'I've applied for Mr Howard's next registrar position,' Mike, the SHO told her. 'I probably haven't got much of a chance, though. It's the same problem—loads of competition already and neither registrar job's available till August.'

'*Neither* job?' Claire blinked. 'Does that mean Lisa is leaving?'

'With any luck.' Mike took a mouthful of his beer, exchanging a look she couldn't decipher with his house officer over his polystyrene cup. 'No guarantees, though. She might be appointed again.'

'Can they do that?' She looked at them both, warming even more towards the two men now she'd sensed that they were not exactly enamoured with the other woman. 'When I worked here hospital training positions were strictly for six months, rarely extended.'

'Lisa's now specialising in vascular,' Mike explained, mentioning Ben's speciality. Although Ben covered general surgery as well when he was on call, most of his time was devoted to vascular surgery, which was surgery involving blood vessels, as well as including some organ transplant work. 'Her first six months on his team formed part of her general training and these six months are part of her specialist training. That time could easily be extended.'

Their gloomy expressions made her smile faintly, pleased that at least she was not the only one dismayed by the prospect. Obviously Lisa didn't consider her juniors warranted the full charm treatment.

'Speaking of you know who...' Mike's gaze swung to the far entrance where Lisa was just arriving, with her gleaming hair immaculately coiled and looking elegant despite the limitations of the white doctor's coat she wore. She was accepting a drink from Duncan Allbright.

'Uh, oh,' he continued softly, as Lisa looked straight towards them, then seemed to murmur an excuse and start in their direction. 'Here comes trouble. Wonder what we've done this time?'

'We're enjoying ourselves,' his house officer muttered. 'That's probably enough.'

Tensing, Claire joined the two men in watching Lisa's smooth approach.

'Michael, I see Mr Sykes is still on the ward,' Lisa said crisply, her gaze merely flickering over Claire as if she was not worth even a greeting—making Claire's nerves clench tighter. 'Wouldn't your time be better employed seeing to his discharge than wasted socialising?'

'We couldn't get transport today,' Mike said quietly. 'It's arranged for tomorrow morning.'

'Can't his relatives take him?'

'His wife doesn't drive and there's no one else,' he explained. 'A son in Bristol but that's all.'

'He's too frail for a cab,' his house officer said quickly, when Lisa opened her mouth as if to argue. 'We thought another night wouldn't do any harm—'

'I need the bed,' Lisa snapped. 'Ben asked me to admit someone he saw in clinic today for his list tomorrow. I've organised for him to come to the ward tonight.'

The two men looked at each other. 'We could discharge Mr Lee,' Mike said hesitantly. 'He's made arrangements to go tomorrow but his wife comes every night to see him. If we let her know she could bring his things—'

'See to it.' Lisa clapped her hands. 'Off you go. One of you will have to stay to admit the new man since the on-call people never do it properly. Make sure all his results are in his notes for the morning.'

'I'll do it.' The house officer's tone was resigned but both doctors exchanged speaking looks, before nodding farewell to Claire and leaving.

Before Claire could make an equally quick retreat Lisa's gaze swung to her. 'Dr Marshall.'

'Lisa.' Claire managed a pale smile. 'Things sound busy on the ward.'

'As they are always,' the other woman said. 'After a career in general practice I imagine you've forgotten how it feels to work under pressure.'

'You'd be surprised,' Claire said tightly, meeting Lisa's supercilious stare with a frosty one of her own. 'Of course I don't have any juniors to...run around after me.'

'But, then, checking children's throats and prescribing tranquillisers is hardly demanding,' the younger woman drawled, her sharpened gaze suggesting she'd taken Claire's inference. 'Surgery is very different.'

Claire's grip tightened on the cup she held. 'I hear your time with Ben is almost over. Found a new job yet?'

Lisa's eyes narrowed. 'I wouldn't believe everything you hear, Dr Marshall. Rumours have a way of getting away on themselves.'

'Ready, Claire?' Ben's arm slid around her stiff waist and made her catch her breath. Preoccupied with deflecting Lisa's bitchiness, she hadn't heard his approach.

'I thought we'd leave,' he said smoothly. 'Lisa, everything all right with Mr Simpson's admission?'

'I've arranged everything,' Lisa said with a smile which, Claire thought, could have lit the whole of Hammersmith. But then her eyes dropped to the hand at Claire's waist and Claire saw the smile falter momentarily. 'You're not leaving now are you?' the registrar continued, looking at Ben now and ignoring Claire again. 'I'd like to discuss tomorrow's list.'

'Everything's sorted and I'll be in early,' Ben said dismissively, his arm tightening again on Claire's waist as if he'd sensed her desire to escape. 'Ready, darling?'

She wasn't, and she was startled by the endearment, but his cool expression suggested that how she felt was irrelevant. With the heat of his arm burning through her dress and turning her legs weak, she murmured something vague in Lisa's direction, conscious of the other woman's icy stare at her back as she let Ben steer her to the door.

When they drove past the intersection where he

should have turned left to go to the surgery so she could collect her car she roused enough from the turmoil of her thoughts to send him a questioning look.

'I'll drive you tomorrow,' he said tightly.

'Really, there's no need—'

'There's every need,' he countered. 'You're not going back there tonight.' They had stopped at lights and his dark gaze swung briefly to her then away again.

At the house she didn't move until he opened the door for her.

When they were inside, with the burglar alarm disabled, he leaned back against the closed door, regarding her darkly.

'I had no idea he felt like that,' she said defensively, her voice shaky as she acknowledged the cause of his mood and so spoke of David. 'He's confused. He's only been separated from Rebecca since Christmas. We're close and he's vulnerable.'

'What did he say?'

'That...that he cared for me.'

'You're my wife.'

'And you're my husband,' she protested, backing away. 'Be honest. Did that matter to you?'

Ben swore. His face set now, he came for her—caught her even though she tried to escape. Effortlessly he swung her struggling body across his shoulder and marched towards the stairs. 'That's enough,' he said rawly. 'No more.'

'Put me down!' She hammered her fists against his back but he was big and powerful and her protests were as ineffectual as her blows. 'What are you doing?'

'What the hell do you think?' He carried her into his room, dumped her onto his bed and came after her. His hands went to the buttons at the front of her dress. 'One guess, Claire. Hmm? One guess.'

'Stop it.' She snatched at his hands, tried to stop him, but he was too strong for her and his determined fingers

tore at her clothes. 'Not like this,' she gasped. 'Ben...not
in anger.'

'I'm not angry at you.' He shifted, slid down her and
buried his mouth in the side of her neck, sending waves
of startling heat across her half-bared skin. 'Only at myself.' He captured her mouth, rubbed her, grazed her lips.
'I should have done this sooner. Stop fighting—it won't
make any difference.' His hands still worked at her
clothes. 'Let me.'

But the dark flush across his cheekbones, the vivid,
glitter that darkened his eyes as his seeking hands parted
lacy cups to get at her breasts, told her that this wasn't
some cold, calculated punishment. He wanted her, she
realised faintly, genuinely wanted her. 'Lisa,' she
groaned, twisting her head. 'No. I don't want this.'

'You don't know what you want.' His hands slid beneath her buttocks and, as if to prove him right, her body
arched as if welcoming his touch, letting him tug free
the crumpled dress and the fragile cotton at her hips.
'Stop thinking.' His voice was hoarse. 'Feel.'

But she did feel, that was the trouble—that was why
she was finding it so hard to resist him. It had been too
long and his touch was reawakening a craving for him
she'd rather she kept under control. Physically, it would
be easy to give in, and if he'd asked her yesterday she
knew she'd have done so, but now there was too much
unresolved between them again to allow her to surrender
emotionally.

But then she weakened. If the physical closeness led
to them being able to talk...afterwards, if they could
really talk... 'Ben...please, promise me—'

'No promises.' Leaving her dress bunched at her feet,
he came up to her, his mouth hot on her neck. 'For God's
sake, Claire, for once stop fighting me.'

Stop fighting. No more fighting. That was what she
wanted, wasn't it? She wanted peace again. She desperately wanted everything between them to be the way it

had been before things had become so complicated. They'd always been good in bed together. Perhaps this was the best place to begin trying to make things better?

Wordlessly she lifted her hands to his back and, as if sensing her surrender, his eyes darkened approvingly and he moved abruptly to straddle her thighs. He bent over her but Claire rose to meet him. Suddenly determined to share his passion, she lifted her shoulders from the bed, her fingers grasping at his back.

Then it was easy. She kissed him as he'd kissed her, short, tight, passionate kisses that made her ache, and she slid her tongue against his, abruptly mad for the aroused male taste of him, her movements unconsciously paralleling the deeper rhythm she craved.

'All right,' she whispered, her hands sliding from his shoulders lower, beneath his shirt. She separated the cloth from his belt then spread her hands urgently across the hard, sweat-sheened heat of his back. The short crescents of her nails bit into him, grasped him, but she wanted more. 'Ben...now, please. Quickly.'

His eyes glinted with a brief, harsh satisfaction but he pushed her back against the covers and said nothing. Determined hands went to her breasts, cupped them, squeezed her while he watched her gasp—and then he lowered his mouth and licked her, grazing then sucking hard, until her eyes shut and her head turned frantically back and forth against the pillows and she wanted to scream.

Abruptly he shifted. She felt brief coolness when he separated her thighs then the slight pause as he adjusted his clothing before he surged into her waiting tightness in fierce and silent possession.

It was quick but she needed little more and her body shivered in release as he tensed above her.

Seconds later, while she still gasped for breath, he began to move again, more slowly this time—slowly, more deeply, harder, bringing her now to a deep, shuddering peak that left her body aching and slick with sweat.

He hadn't spoken, not a word, and when she opened her eyes, wanting reassurance, his hand shifted to her mouth, covered it gently and held it closed as if to stop her words while his mouth lowered to the side of her neck. To her astonishment, when she thought she could bear no more, she felt her body begin to loosen again.

But he pulled away abruptly and she rolled to stare at him, her breath coming faster when she saw that he'd merely stood to strip off his clothes, his rising arousal telling her he wasn't leaving her.

They made love again and then he let her sleep, only to wake her after what seemed like scant minutes, his mouth at her hip. It was still dark and he must have pulled the blinds for there was no light from the street. She could see nothing and feel nothing but him and she grasped his hair, abruptly aroused, and her breath rasped in and out of her chest as he pleasured her again.

Then she let him swing her over until she straddled him and, encouraged by his arousal, she teased him until once again he pulled her down and took control.

In the morning he took her into the shower and lathered her and soaped her with gentle fingers that probed the part of her that ached from the night before until nothing mattered again but his touch, and he entered her and made love to her while the water cascaded over her up-turned face and across her breasts and down into the junction between them.

Still he hadn't spoken and there were only the soft sounds of her gasps and the noise of the water and his movements, and the deeper silence lingered until it was too late for her to speak.

He washed her clean again and guided her to her bedroom.

Her body was sore and she found herself lazy and

tired and, as if she were a child, she let him dress her. He selected her underwear carefully, throwing aside the sensible, cotton garments she favoured and finding the silk he'd given her years before.

She couldn't suppress her shiver at the cool glide of the fragile fabric against her skin, and his fingers brushed deliberately over the taut imprint of her nipples while he watched her face, seeming to enjoy her reaction.

She stepped into the underwear he'd chosen and he let the cloth linger briefly against her thighs, as if warming it before tugging it higher. He had her stand there, flushed and already aroused again, while he walked around her, inspected her, but instead of making love to her again he simply brought her a dress, slid it over her head and fastened and buttoned her until she was covered.

Then he took her to the dressing-table and she sat at the stool while he stood behind her, smoothing her hair, their eyes locked in their reflections. Hers she saw were dazed, bewildered, but his remained unreadable.

Her arms felt heavy and languid but she managed to lift them, her movements mechanical as she brushed on her make-up, fastened small pearl earrings and did all the things she needed to do. 'Ben, there's so much... We have to talk.'

'Later.' He took her to work—no time for breakfast or study—and stopped in the car park. Leaving the engine running, he came around to her side, tugged her out, then pressed her back against the car so that the cold of the metal seeped through her dress and fought with the heat from his touch as he kissed her so thoroughly that he left her aching anew.

Apparently uncaring that they could have been seen by anybody who happened to look out of the surgery's main window, he stepped back, tugged her upright again and gave her her briefcase.

Wordlessly he returned to the car and drove away leaving her staring after him breathless and bemused.

Warren's raised eyebrows when she drifted into the surgery suggested he'd either witnessed the episode or noticed her confusion. 'What's happened?' he barked. 'Won the lottery?'

'I don't have a ticket.' She frowned at him, trying to recoup—trying to remember how she was supposed to be behaving. 'Er, I shouldn't be here, should I? I should be on my calls.'

'Here's your list,' he confirmed, passing her a short computer printout with just one additional hand-printed name and address at the bottom. 'Only four today, lucky you.' He frowned when she made no move to leave. 'Claire?'

She blinked at him. 'Hmm?'

'Work,' he offered. 'Remember? A job you do that pays us all money?'

'Yes.' She smiled then. 'Thanks. Of course.' Clutching the printout, she turned around and went back to the car park, moving slowly and wincing slightly with the discomfort from muscles that until last night had been little used recently.

Only when she saw David's car come in behind her did she remember the day before. 'Oh, God,' she mumbled, descending abruptly back to earth. She got out of her car again and went to speak to him.

He'd obviously been up all night—he looked terrible. 'I'm sorry,' he said jerkily, coming to meet her halfway. 'I embarrassed you yesterday.'

'You didn't embarrass me,' she said quietly.

'Ben? He didn't...he wasn't angry with you? He didn't...say anything?'

'No.' Claire frowned at him, not understanding what he meant. 'David, I'm worried. Are you all right?'

'I need a holiday,' he admitted. He ran his palm down his pale face, held his chin for a few seconds and then let the hand slip so that it dangled at his side awkwardly, as if he didn't know what to do with it. 'Warren called me at home last night,' he told her, his red-rimmed and bloodshot eyes sliding away from her gaze. 'God knows how he knew I was upset but he suggested I take a holiday,' he said roughly. 'Apparently I've been looking "tired"…' he held up curled fingers to illustrate quotation marks '…lately. He said he had a locum available for a few weeks, starting Monday. What do you think?'

'That it's a good idea.' As far as she could remember, he hadn't taken a decent break in two years—he'd stayed working all through the time surrounding his separation. It was little wonder he was so strained. It was obvious he desperately needed time away—immediately—before he spiralled into some sort of emotional breakdown. 'David, you don't really…?'

'No.' His eyes ducked her concerned gaze again. 'No, you're right,' he muttered. 'I did some hard thinking last night. I'm still mixed up over Rebecca. You're a friend and you're there and I thought you and Ben were having problems,' he said finally, looking up at her. 'I saw him with his registrar and she's a beautiful woman and I assumed they were having an affair. In my subconscious I think I thought it was an easy solution.'

'There aren't any easy solutions,' she said quietly, despite her relief that he was being rational about what had happened, feeling cold inside. Obviously he *had* seen more than Ben and Lisa merely dining together.

'I know. But don't worry about me.' He smiled—a strained smile, she noted, but still a smile. 'Last night…that isn't the way I really feel.'

'That's a relief,' she admitted. 'I'm not…well, Ben and I, we're…happy,' she said carefully.

'If you say so.' He sagged slightly. 'But if ever that changes…?'

Claire looked at him sharply but he just shrugged, a vaguely deprecatory gesture that didn't reassure her.

'Thanks for talking,' he said quietly. He trudged past her towards the surgery. 'See you later.'

'OK.' But as she looked towards the surgery she saw that Warren was watching them from the window, his frown suggesting that he'd witnessed the encounter. Claire grimaced, wondering what was going through his head. It wasn't unusual for her to converse privately with David but that conversation had been intense. From a distance they'd probably looked very intimate. Which would have seemed doubly odd if Warren had also witnessed Ben's uncharacteristically possessive embrace minutes before.

Telling herself that there was little point in worrying about things she couldn't change, she started the car and backed out of the parking space.

On her way back from her calls she stopped in to see Susan Drury, her patient who'd been newly released from St Paul's Hospital to a halfway house not far from the surgery. But she hadn't phoned ahead and the dishevelled woman who came to the door told her that Susan had caught a bus to go to a job centre. 'She's looking hard for work,' she told Claire. 'I don't know when she'll be back. Yesterday she was gone all day.'

Pleased at Susan's initiative, Claire left a message saying that she'd called to say hello and wishing her luck with her job hunt.

In the afternoon Wendy called. Claire had assumed that Wendy would be returning to London that day, although she'd arranged for her mother to collect Jamie again that afternoon just in case, but Wendy was phoning from York. 'I tried all last night to call the house,' she said. 'Sure the phone wasn't off the hook?'

'Er...I suppose it might have been,' Claire conceded, realising that anything was possible, Ben perhaps having decided he wanted no distractions. 'When are we going to see you?'

But it seemed they weren't. Wendy had found a job

in York, helping behind the bar at a local pub, and she'd decided not to come back to London. 'Mum needs help around the house,' Wendy told her. 'The doctor said she won't be able to do much after the hysterectomy. Tell Jamie I miss him, but sorry, Claire. You'll find someone else easily enough—he's an angel.'

'I understand.' Although she sighed inwardly she understood Wendy's desire to stay close to her mother. She promised to pack up the rest of Wendy's things and send them up, along with the holiday pay she was due. 'I hope your mum gets better quickly.'

When she had a gap in her list she called an employment agency she'd used in the past in emergencies. 'We don't have any formally qualified nannies available now,' she was told. 'But by the end of the term we should have one or two on our books. Can you wait? Or shall I send résumés from some of the au pairs we have?'

'Résumés would be good.' Claire nodded her thanks for the computer-generated set of repeat prescriptions one of the receptionists brought in for her at the moment. 'I can't wait till the end of term. Would you fax them, please?' She tucked the phone into her neck, leaving her hands free to check through and sign each prescription. 'It's urgent that I find someone as soon as possible.'

After clinic the partners met briefly to discuss a recent audit that Warren had asked David to perform on the practice's management of specialist referrals. There were four partners—herself, Warren and David, all working full time, and Martin, who was a single parent with three young children and worked only two days a week, not at all during the school holidays and who carried no on-call responsibilities.

But instead of the detailed analysis of statistics their audits normally involved David's presentation was sketchy. Obviously, Claire realised, he'd been too busy to do much more than tackle the subject superficially.

Warren's assessment, though, seemed less generous.

He didn't say anything but he sent David a disapproving tight-lipped look, before discussing points David had not included.

Because of the limitations of the research it was difficult to come to any conclusions, and in the discussion that followed they all agreed to make an effort to keep notes about how often and for what reasons they sought specialist opinions so they would have more to discuss at a future meeting.

After that the talk turned to generalities, but when they were starting to pack up Warren said, 'There's a clinical assistant post going at the hospital. Surgery, including ENT, which would be useful experience for one of you. One day a week involving outpatients with occasional day surgery. Claire, you've done a bit of surgery in the past. Interested?'

'It would be good experience,' she mused. The part-time hospital position, the sort frequently held by GPs seeking further training—would be excellent training, training which would benefit the practice. Considering how many consultations involved ear, nose and throat surgery, she was very interested. 'What about my work here?' she ventured. 'One day a week's a big chunk of time to be away. How does everyone else feel?'

'Martin's decided he can add a day,' Warren said firmly, and Martin nodded his agreement.

'Not during school holidays, of course,' the younger man added, 'but I can cover Thursdays otherwise.'

'And things will be quieter in the holidays, anyway,' Warren said, as if everything was settled. 'They always are. In September we'll have a new trainee but, if necessary, the income from the hospital work will help towards financing a locum.'

'I suppose I could apply,' Claire said slowly. 'There's no guarantee I'd get the job.'

'Nothing to lose.' Warren was obviously pleased. 'Now, David's taking leave from the weekend.' To

Claire's puzzlement, behind his spectacles his round eyes blinked at her. 'I've already spoken with Katie Saunders,' he continued, 'and she's happy to cover as long as you want, David, so I urge you to consider taking all the time you're due. You deserve it, given how long it's been since your last break. So,' he rubbed his hands together 'everything's settled, then.' He looked around at them all expectantly. 'Unless there're any objections?'

'None.' Claire shook her head. Warren seemed to have been busy, she thought idly, more than a little surprised. An excellent general practitioner, he was usually more lackadaisical about the administrative side of his role. Still, she reasoned, the clinical assistant post had probably been mentioned to him by one of his contacts, and he clearly realised that David needed a holiday and so for once had worked quickly to make sure it eventuated. She was impressed. And David, she saw, looked relieved that things had been organised so quickly.

Katie Saunders had covered Warren's last holiday, she remembered, and would be covering his summer holiday this year as well. An older woman with adult children and a fanatical interest in gardening, the capable GP had retired from her own practice and now did only part-time locum work to allow her more time for her plants.

Claire's legs still felt stiff as she walked out to the car park and she flushed as she let herself remember the reason for her muscle weariness.

But later, coming home late after her teaching session at the university, she felt more than mildly embarrassed. Heated to the point of discomfort and more than a little anxious, she'd already noted that Ben's study light was on before she let herself into the house.

The night before had been their most passionate night together in years but they still hadn't spoken about any of the issues that blighted their relationship. What did he intend to happen now?

CHAPTER SIX

BEN had clearly heard her because he was halfway down the stairs when Claire opened the front door. His suit suggesting that he'd only recently arrived home himself, he looked every inch the powerful lover of the night before and she met his dark, enigmatic regard and flushed violently.

'Hi,' she said huskily, hearing herself sound like a nervous teenager. 'Have you just got home? What about Jamie?'

'Still at your mother's.'

'I thought you were going to collect him?'

He followed her into the kitchen where she turned on the kettle to boil water for coffee. 'There was an emergency,' he explained, 'as I was due to leave. I had to operate. Jamie was already asleep when I called and Esme suggested he stay.'

'Oh.' She blinked, surprised that he hadn't called her when the emergency had arisen. Normally he'd have expected her to organise Jamie's care. 'Thank you. Oh.' She looked at him quickly, still self-conscious, remembering the things they'd done the night before, the way he'd touched her. 'Wendy rang. She's staying in York.' She explained about the agency, her voice still jerky. 'It might take a while to find someone.'

Ben lifted one shoulder, then sat on a stool at the breakfast bar while she poured them each a drink. 'We'll work something out,' he said calmly, and she looked up sharply, startled that he'd not suggested she take time off work—normally his knee-jerk response in crises like this.

90

'I should finish early tomorrow,' he continued. 'I'll cover while you're on call.'

'That would help.' She passed him his coffee, which was black with no sugar—unlike hers, which she preferred milky and sweet. She had Thursday night off, as well as the weekend, so she could look after Jamie then, as long as Mary was happy to collect him after school. She'd ask her mother to stay over on Friday night unless Ben was free. He'd be on call at the weekend so would probably not be around.

'I—I'm applying for a clinical assistant post,' she said between sips, nervously covering the silence that had risen between them. 'Surgery and ENT. Thursdays. What do you think?'

'The experience will be useful.'

'Do you know who it'll be with?' As a senior surgeon at the hospital it was likely he did. 'Which consultants, I mean?'

'ENT, probably Joe Pritchard,' he told her, his attention now on his drink. 'For surgery, could be any one of a number of consultants.'

Claire nodded, pleased at least about Joe. She'd met him on several occasions and often referred patients to him. He was a pleasant man, always happy to help. 'Of course I might not get the job,' she conceded.

'Are you asking me to apply pressure?'

'No, of course not.' She lowered her cup abruptly, spilling a little of the coffee in her shock. 'Absolutely not.' She met his dark gaze unflinchingly. 'That wasn't what I meant.' She reached clumsily for a cloth and dabbed at the spill. 'You know that.'

'Do I?' He regarded her steadily, seeming to contemplate that. 'You've obviously decided you want the position.'

'Not unethically,' she said abruptly, awkward again. She wrung out the cloth at the sink and hung it over the tap to dry. 'Not over other candidates.'

'If you say so.' His coffee finished, he levered himself from the stool and took his cup to the sink and rinsed it. But instead of walking away he moved behind her where she stood against the bench, his breath stirring her hair as he took her cup firmly from her shaking hands and pushed it away. 'Hungry?'

'No.' She tipped her head back, her eyes closing as his hands slid around her waist and then up to cup her tightening breasts. 'Ben, I...'

But she didn't know the words for what worried her. Last night had re-established the sexual side of their relationship with an intensity that was still with her, but now she realised that what she most craved from him was intimacy, the close sharing of feelings and emotions which had once bound them together so tightly. They'd lost that somehow and had still not found it again.

Now that the edge had been taken off their desire they should be talking, exploring each other's minds again, not simply their bodies. She needed to know what was going to happen. She needed reassurance that even if he no longer loved her as he had there was still security, reassurance that she was important to him for more than sex.

But, as if he sensed her doubts, Ben's hands became suddenly more urgent, tempting her and weakening her with their knowing caresses. He turned her, hushing her. 'Shh, Claire. Don't think.' He lifted her effortlessly so that she sat on the cool granite, then shifted against her, his mouth warm at her forehead, her eyes, her cheek and finally her mouth. 'Only this,' he murmured, his hands busy at her clothes. 'Just this.'

And she let him dissolve her with his touch, too aroused now to have the strength to fight him when he was so intent.

He carried her to his bedroom and made love to her but when they turned over, spoon-like, breathless and damp, his mouth at her neck, soothing her, the telephone rang.

With a groan he rolled away from her and answered it. There was a brief discussion about a patient and then he said, 'Ten minutes.' He replaced the receiver.

She felt him leave the bed and rolled over, holding the sheet to her breasts. 'Why you?' she said faintly. 'You're not on call.'

'It's the man I operated on earlier,' he said quietly, at the wardrobe, pulling jeans over the hard strength of the thighs she'd felt so recently against her. 'He's bleeding, possibly leaking from his repair. I'm the best qualified to go back in.'

'Oh.' She rolled back, her greedy wish to have him close all night immediately seeming selfish. Ben's work was vital and she understood that. That was the way it had always been with him and, in truth, his dedication was one of the things she admired most about him.

She heard him finish dressing then he knelt on the bed, tugged the sheet down and pressed a hard kiss to her shoulder. 'Go to sleep,' he ordered. 'This might take hours.'

But she found herself fully awake and after hearing his car leave—fighting the urge to stay in the sheets that still bore his scent—she wriggled out of bed and straightened the bedclothes. Although he bore no signs of it, he had to be tired from the near sleepless night before, she reasoned. And two nights without sleep would affect even him. The last thing he needed was to find her in his bed when he got home, possibly only an hour or two before he had to leave for work again. He'd need sleep, not her, and he wouldn't want to talk.

Back in her own bed she slept restlessly and woke later than she'd wanted to the next morning. When she emerged from a hurried shower she saw that Ben's door was open but the bedding was disturbed, suggesting that he had made it home at some stage but had already gone again.

She rang her mother and spoke to a cheerful Jamie, who reassured her that he'd had a terrific time, playing with Rex and eating all sorts of treats that she normally tried to ration.

'Daddy called me,' he told her, 'from his hospital. He's very busy,' he said proudly.

'I know, darling.' She found herself wishing Ben had found time to ring her as well, then told herself she was being unreasonable. He hadn't seen Jamie since Monday morning and it was natural that he'd want to speak with his son.

Warren came to her office first thing. 'That clinical assistant post's in the bag,' he told her.

Claire swung around from the cupboard where she'd been stowing her briefcase, startled. 'But I haven't even filled in an application.'

'No other applicants.' He beamed. 'They need someone immediately and since the only interest has been from us the position's yours. You start tomorrow. Eight-thirty. Main Outpatients.'

Claire blinked. 'That soon?'

'I've talked with Martin,' Warren continued. 'He'll be here to cover your calls and clinic. You'll be working for Joe Pritchard.'

He made as if to leave but Claire said quickly, still surprised by her partner's new-found organisational skills, 'Joe Pritchard's ENT. Which general surgeon will I be working for?'

Warren's hand clenched the doorhandle, his brow furrowed. 'Is that important?' he asked gravely.

'Not especially.' But she frowned at him, puzzled by his tone and by the faint flush that darkened his apple-red cheeks. 'Warren, it's not—?'

'Busy. Busy,' he announced, peering out into the waiting-room. 'Sorry, Claire, better leave you to it.'

As he'd predicted, it was a busy day. David and Warren, who both covered the obstetric duties in the practice, shared a morning clinic which meant she dealt with any urgent problems from their lists involving non-obstetric illnesses.

The past three days had been stormy and warm and that added to all the spring pollen floating around, seemed to have triggered an outbreak of allergic reactions and asthma in the district. There'd also been adverse publicity in the papers and television about one particular antihistamine suggesting that it had been implicated in deaths from heart problems. Consequently, several of the patients she saw came simply because they were worried about the medication, one which they normally simply purchased over the counter.

'It's only a problem if there's pre-existing heart disease,' Claire reassured the third patient to question the popular drug, wishing the media had outlined the details more plainly and so reduced the alarm among her patients. She'd been aware of the potential problems with that particular type of antihistamine and had consequently never recommended it for patients at risk but with all the headlines it was unsurprising that other people were frightened.

'When people have the sort of heart disease that sometimes needs a pacemaker, it can make that condition worse, but it can't cause problems in the first place.' But to allay their anxieties she recommended another tablet.

Over lunch, determined to keep their conversation neutral once she discovered he was the only other person in the kitchen, she told David about the cases she'd seen that morning.

'Not surprising,' he countered. 'Nine months after that last Pill scare we had more deliveries than in the previous five months added together.'

She returned his pale smile unreservedly, pleased that the awkwardness between them was fading. She was fond of him and the last year had been difficult for him. She didn't want their friendship damaged by embarrassment about what had happened. 'This time there'll just be people sneezing,' she joked. 'Time to buy shares in tissue-making companies.'

The door to the kitchen opened and Warren poked his head in, his smile fading as he saw them both there. 'Ah, David,' he said carefully. 'A word, please. In my office. Bring your lunch—this might take a while.'

David looked at Claire and frowned slightly, as if annoyed by the interruption, but after only the faintest of delays he followed Warren out of the room.

Later, before leaving for the evening, David came to see her in her office. 'One of my patients might call you out tonight,' he advised, handing her the file. 'Seventeen-year-old student. Normally mild asthma, no hospital admissions, but she hasn't been good today. She came up this afternoon and needed the nebuliser but felt well enough afterwards to go home. I've started steroids and told her to increase her inhaler but she might call tonight if she's not improving.'

'Fine.' Claire nodded her understanding. 'Peak flow?'

'Never normally bothers,' he told her. 'Today she's blowing 310 before and 340 afterwards, which isn't too bad but obviously less than I'd expect. I don't know what she's been like lately.'

'OK.' She tilted her head, smiled gently. 'Any idea where you're going for your holiday?'

He looked at her with a sharpness that puzzled her. 'Holiday?'

'Your leave,' she prompted. 'Next week.'

'Oh.' His face relaxed slightly although his eyes remained watchful. 'Haven't made up my mind,' he admitted. 'Not entirely. There're a lot of things to think about.'

Her door, already ajar, was suddenly pushed wider, and Warren was there. 'Ah,' he said heavily, his eyes darting between them. 'David. Mind if I have a word with Claire? Won't take long.'

'I'm leaving, anyway.' His tone seemed oddly tinged with impatience, Claire thought as David collected his case and left abruptly.

But when they were alone Warren seemed to lose whatever he'd meant to say and he looked at Claire's expectant face blankly for a few seconds, murmured something vague about it not being anything that couldn't wait and left, leaving her staring after him.

In keeping with the day, her evening was busy and her clinic full so she didn't finish until after nine-thirty, then she had two house calls straight away. When she was almost home she was bleeped again and she pulled the Audi into a bus stop and used the practice's mobile to answer it.

The call was from the mother of a child with asthma and by the time Claire had driven to see him and given him some nebulised bronchodilator, which quickly improved his wheezing, it was after eleven.

She arrived home shortly after. From the lights she knew Ben must be in his study but she crept into the other bedroom to see Jamie. He was asleep, his eyelashes long and shadowed against his soft cheek, and didn't stir when she crouched and kissed him.

Ben was watching her from the doorway when she straightened. 'I didn't have time to call before bedtime,' she whispered. 'How is he?'

'Exhausted from two nights with Rex,' he said quietly. 'And, if Jamie's exhausted, imagine how Rex is,' he added, more normally now that she'd followed him away from the bedroom. 'Not to mention your mother. Have you eaten?'

'A few biscuits.' She followed him downstairs, deliberately not allowing herself to check the banister for the dust she knew must have accumulated since the small effort she'd made several weeks before.

The one fax she'd received from the agency that day had been for an applicant who didn't speak English and although the agency person had assured her that for extra money the girl would be happy to help with housework, Claire had quickly decided she wouldn't be suitable. Help with Jamie's schoolwork at this stage was more important than household chores.

In the kitchen now, Ben opened the fridge. 'Cheddar sandwich all right? There doesn't seem to be much else.'

'Sorry.' She grimaced, remembering that she hadn't shopped properly for ages. 'A sandwich is fine, thank you,' she said huskily not arguing when he waved her away as she tried to help, appreciating his thoughtfulness. She sat wearily on the edge of one of the stools at the breakfast bar. 'I should have time to go to the supermarket tomorrow.'

Usually a comment like that would have provoked some sort of pointed remark about her working hours but although she tensed herself Ben stayed quiet.

'I got the hospital job,' she said huskily, a few minutes later when it seemed no remark would be forthcoming. 'I start tomorrow.'

'We can meet for lunch,' he said quietly, passing her the prepared sandwich, his mouth tightening fractionally as he saw how eagerly she reached for the food. 'At one.'

'I'll call your office,' she said between mouthfuls. In the beginning, years ago when they'd first met and had both been working at the hospital, they'd lunched together most days. 'I don't know my timetable for the day.'

He poured her some milk, and slid the glass across the granite towards her. 'Do you have to go out again tonight?'

'Not that I know about.' But she shifted on her stool, discomfited by his regard. 'It's been busy, though, so I'll probably be called.' Her bleeper promptly shrilled and she grimaced at him. This late it had to be work.

It was the mother of Angela Dunning, the patient whom David had seen earlier with asthma. 'She's very breathless,' Mrs Dunning told her. 'She's using her inhaler but it isn't helping any more. What should I do?'

'I'll come straight away.' Claire replaced the phone and looked at Ben. 'Sorry.'

'It's your job.'

'Thanks for the sandwich.' She collected her bag. 'See you tomorrow.'

Angela looked significantly worse than she'd sounded from David's description. Her pulse was over a hundred and she was audibly wheezy, barely managing to blow 250 on the peak flow meter.

She'd taken the prednisolone tablets David had prescribed for her but as yet they hadn't improved things. 'Her breathing's worse,' her mother said tightly, as Angela hunched over the nebuliser, which was spraying salbutamol into her lungs.

'The medication I've put in there will help relax your airways,' Claire explained soothingly, wanting Angela to stay calm.

Five minutes after the solution ran out Claire rechecked Angela's lungs which remained wheezy, then asked her to use the peak flow meter again. 'Two-seventy,' she said slowly, checking the measurement. Then she handed her back the little device. 'Best of three.'

But 270 was the highest of them all and Claire opened another vial of salbutamol into the machine. While it bubbled she asked Angela's mother about risk factors.

'No pets, and I'm very careful about dusting,' she was told. 'I use low-allergy bedding and we've got one of those new vacuum cleaners—you know, the filter ones that take all the dust away completely.'

'It's probably the weather.' Claire explained how the

heat created layers in the atmosphere and trapped irritating particles close to the ground where they could be breathed in.

When there was no improvement in Angela's peak flow after the second nebuliser treatment, Claire rang the hospital. She spoke to the on-call medical registrar, a helpful-sounding doctor who told her to send Angela to Accident and Emergency.

'We may not end up admitting her,' he said, 'but we'll keep an eye on her for a few hours and make sure there's plenty of improvement before we send her home.'

Next morning Claire called at Casualty on her way to Outpatients, and the receptionist told her that Angela had been properly admitted shortly after her arrival.

Claire called the surgery, knowing that David would want to know. 'I've made a note of the ward so I'll pop in and see her if I get a few minutes,' she told him.

She spent the morning in ENT clinic with Joe Pritchard. 'The greatest thing about hospital practice is that you GPs have already screened the referrals,' he told her. 'You won't see plain old ordinary sore throats, the sort of ones you must see every day yourself in your own surgery, or at least you shouldn't see any here.'

It was a busy clinic, with more than ninety patients to see, but manageable because Joe had two registrars working for him, as well as an SHO and two enthusiastic medical students who drifted from room to room, depending on which doctor summoned them. Each of the other doctors in the clinic saw patients on their own— with the exception of Claire, who sat in with Joe for this first session—referring problems to him as appropriate.

They didn't finish until one-thirty. Claire telephoned Ben's secretary in case he was still about but he answered the phone himself and told her to come up to his office.

'I haven't long,' she said quickly, when she got there. 'I think I'm supposed to be at a surgical clinic by two.'

'You have to eat.' He tossed her a plastic wedge containing two salad sandwiches covered with Cellophane. 'And you're not in a clinic this afternoon. As part of the government's waiting list initiative, we do an extra day-surgery list once a month and today's it. You're in Theatre.'

Midway through opening the food she froze. 'What are you saying?'

'You're working for me, Claire.' Something dark in his expression showed her that her shocked reaction satisfied him. 'I'm your new boss.'

CHAPTER SEVEN

'LISA works in one theatre while I cover the other,' Ben continued smoothly. 'Today you're assisting with my list.'

'Why didn't you tell me?' Claire protested, reeling. 'Last night. Even the night before when you asked if I wanted you to pull strings. Why didn't you tell me then?'

'Would you have wanted the job?'

She hesitated, unsure. 'I don't know.'

'It's good for you to get away from the practice for a day. It'll help you keep your sense of perspective. And you'll enjoy this—you always liked surgery.'

Was he saying he'd offered this position to help her? But that didn't make sense. Why? 'Perhaps,' she admitted. 'But there was no need to keep it a secret.' Then she frowned, suddenly chilled. Didn't it make more sense that appointing her was part of some horrible game he was playing with Lisa? Perhaps he'd told Lisa that he wasn't prepared to leave his family but perhaps she hadn't believed him. Perhaps bringing her to work with the younger woman was his forceful way of making her confront that.

But, then, this was a hospital-funded position. She could believe him to be ruthless but not unethical. He couldn't have known she'd get the job. 'Who decided?' she demanded. 'Who decided the job was mine?'

'Warren must have told you.'

'He said I was the only applicant.'

'Well, then.' He lowered his eyes, his expression bored now. 'The position was widely advertised. Eat your sandwich, Claire. I don't want you fainting this afternoon.'

'I never faint.' But she felt faint. Still wondering what on earth was going on, she couldn't let it rest. 'Ben, I don't know about this...'

'Eat.' Firm now, he met her doubtful stare commandingly and she found herself opening the rest of the packet. 'You're here now.' He walked to the window and stared out of it, as if tired of their discussion. 'Too late for second thoughts and there's work to do. When you've finished lunch we'll go to Theatre.'

On their way to the day unit he explained that he'd already visited the patients on both lists. 'They arrive around twelve to give the anaesthetists time to assess them. My normal day session is Tuesday morning but, as I said before, this is a new monthly list.'

Claire's eyes tracked their shadows against the pale wall of the corridor. 'This is strange,' she said faintly, for it felt very, very strange to be walking beside him like this through the hospital.

'Old times,' he said shrewdly, and she nodded, for that was exactly what it was like.

She'd met Ben, then a surgical registrar, when she'd started working for him here in this same hospital as an SHO. During the two years previously she'd done stints in Obstetrics and Accident and Emergency as part of her training for general practice, but had enjoyed the surgical side of those jobs so much that after completing another year in general practice she'd applied for a full six-month surgical position, rather than going directly into working in a practice as she'd been scheduled to do.

She'd wanted to see if a career in surgery might suit her. Ben had been her registrar and much of her time on the wards and in clinics and Theatre had been with him. They'd walked along this same corridor just like this many times before.

Only now everything was different, she told herself.

Then, mere weeks after meeting him, she'd been in the midst of her first affair, madly infatuated and barely able to keep her eyes off him. Now she was a mature, adult woman, successful in her career, married and the mother of a seven-year-old boy.

But it felt eerily similar.

The day unit was new. When she'd worked here there'd been very little day surgery and most procedures she'd seen involving a general anaesthetic had been thought to require an overnight stay.

'Mostly veins this afternoon,' he told her. 'It's a vascular session. Not especially interesting for you but a good reminder of basic techniques.'

'Something I need.' She hadn't been inside a proper operating theatre since she'd stopped working with him. Even a few weeks would give her confidence and Warren had mentioned that he was keen for her to do more minor surgery at the practice. There was definitely demand among their patients for such a move. At a recent audit Martin had calculated that, given the numbers of referrals they each made to surgeons for patients needing or requesting removal of minor lumps and bumps, setting up their own minor-surgery facilities would make both economic and practical sense. This time would give her ideas about the equipment they'd need to purchase, as well as updating her skills and giving her useful practice with excellent supervision and teaching.

Ben introduced her to his theatre staff, including his scrub nurse, Lynn, and a large and bubbly circulating nurse called Molly.

'I do both theatres, darling,' Molly told her cheerfully. 'Lisa's as well. She'll be working next door.'

Claire and Ben donned disposable masks and began to scrub their hands and arms in the basins alongside the theatre, and Claire let herself hope that by now Lisa was too immersed in her own list to intrude.

But the registrar promptly strolled in. Wearing a surgical gown which Claire, abruptly shrewish, decided had to be two sizes too small, she leaned against the stainless-steel basin, smiling up at Ben, the curves of her breasts—considering he was scrubbing—provocatively close to his suds-covered elbows. 'I finished writing my paper,' she said slowly. 'Will you have time to check it tonight? I thought we could—'

'Leave it on my desk,' Ben said curtly, and Claire stiffened, wondering if his abruptness was for her benefit. Even if it was, Claire almost felt sorry for the other woman when she saw Lisa's quick and apparently painful indrawn breath.

'I don't think you know about our new clinical assistant,' Ben added, nodding briskly towards Claire. 'Thursday afternoons from today.'

Lisa wore a mask, as they did, and her eyes widened as she inspected Claire, then narrowed immediately as she recognised her. 'Dr Marshall,' she said coldly, looking sharply at Ben.

'Lisa.' Claire's sympathy evaporated and she nodded a terse return to what she assumed was a greeting.

'It's Claire,' Ben said wearily, not looking at either of them. 'Come on, Lisa, you know that much.'

'Claire.' But the registrar's tone was no warmer. 'How cosy,' she said acidly, and Claire noted the pointed withdrawal of the breasts and the rest of her perfect body from Ben's side.

'Is it?' Claire saw that Ben's regard was tinged with impatience and she was glad that it wasn't directed at her. 'Claire will be working closely with me, but if I'm away or unavailable she'll turn to you for assistance.'

'Of course.' The other woman's reply was meek but Claire hoped that the need for her to rely on Lisa's help would never arise. 'Naturally, that's part of my job.'

'Hmm.' Using his elbows, Ben stopped the water, then held his arms up, letting some of the water run off, before he walked to the trolley that Claire had seen Lynn set up while they'd been washing. 'Back to work, Lisa. You must be needed by now.'

With a narrowed glance back towards Claire, Lisa left, leaving behind a loaded and uncomfortable silence.

Claire turned off her tap and held her elbows up, hands high, waiting for Ben to finish at the trolley.

His hands dry now, he hurled the sterile towels he'd used towards the laundry bag, unbundled his gown and thrust his arms into the green sleeves. Then he snapped on sterile gloves and moved away from the trolley, his eyes dark and narrowed above the green pleats of his mask as he looked at her.

'She's not happy,' Claire said nervously, coming to the trolley—speaking more from the urge to cover the silence than any desire to discuss the other woman. Gingerly she folded a towel, drying first her hands, then sliding the sterile cloth down each arm, careful not to contaminate herself.

Molly came to tie Ben's gown at the back, clicking her tongue and shaking her head. 'That girl,' she clucked. 'Face like thunder this afternoon. What have you been saying to her this time?'

Ben lifted his eyes briefly to the ceiling. 'Same thing I should be saying to you, Molly Brown. Time for work.'

But Molly chuckled, and when Ben moved into the theatre she came across to Claire who was waiting in her gown. 'What gloves, honey?'

'Size six,' Claire told her, the older woman's benignly maternal regard making her feel more like a medical student than an experienced GP. 'Hypo-allergenic, please. The others give me a rash.'

'Now mind you take no notice of that Ben,' Molly instructed, pulling open the pack containing the gloves and letting the contents fall onto the trolley. 'Don't let him bully you in there,' she continued cheerfully. 'And don't start making cow eyes at him like that other one or you'll be out of here with a flea in your ear just the same.'

'Cow eyes?' With one glove partly on, Claire stiffened, staring straight ahead at the wall as Molly tied the back of her gown. 'You mean Lisa?'

'Mad for him she is.' Molly clicked her tongue. 'Mooning after him this past year almost.'

'Molly,' Claire spoke quickly, realising that she had to stop her now or both of them would end up very embarrassed. 'Ben and I are married. I've kept my maiden name for work which is why it's different, but I'm his wife.'

'Oh, you're *that* Claire?' But Molly sounded delighted and Claire heard no trace of embarrassment about what she'd just revealed. 'Please to meet you, honey. How's that little boy of yours? Did he enjoy seeing the dinosaurs last week?'

'He loved them.' Claire concentrated on finishing gloving. 'Did Ben tell you about that?'

'That you were going, but I haven't had a chance to find out how it was,' she confirmed. 'I'm going to take my grandchildren there in the holidays. I think they'll like it, too.'

'I'm sure they will.' Claire turned around. 'Molly...about Lisa?'

'Don't you go fretting.' Molly clicked her tongue again. 'He doesn't take any notice so why should you?'

Claire frowned. 'He doesn't?'

'Of course not. He's a good husband, that one—you don't have to worry. There're some that aren't, mind.' She chuckled again. 'Mine for starters but, then, that's part of life. I had my babies and that was enough for me.'

From the other side of the scrub room someone shouted, and Molly clicked her tongue and bustled away. 'That Lisa's roaring for me,' she said cheerfully. 'You go help your husband, honey. I'll be back.'

Claire walked into the theatre and stood for a few seconds, looking at Ben bent over their first patient's leg. She had a good husband, Molly had said. She'd sounded confident that there was nothing between Ben and Lisa. But, then, Ben would have been discreet so the fact that the hospital staff knew nothing was hardly reassuring. And, if what Molly said was right, why hadn't Ben reassured her when she'd questioned him before Scotland? What about what David had seen? And why wouldn't Ben talk properly to her now?

When she approached the table Ben looked up and nodded for her to take the stool opposite him. He was working on one leg, and the rest of their patient was encased in sterile green guards up to the guard-covered metal frame that separated the anaesthetic field from the surgical one.

'Multiple perforations,' he told her, indicating the marker-pen streaks she assumed he'd made earlier when his patient had been conscious and standing so that the dilated veins were obvious. 'Remember what you're doing?'

'Stab, grab and tie,' she confirmed, admiring the quick, intricate handiwork which had always been his trademark.

'Lynn, scalpel for Claire,' he ordered. 'Start mid-calf,' he told Claire, indicating the mark he meant. 'I'll finish here and come down to meet you.'

It was a straightforward and repetitive procedure and Claire found her fluency returning as she tied knot after knot and grew accustomed to handling the instruments again. She did some occasional suturing at the practice, but it had been a long time since she'd needed to use more precise surgical tools.

Although he'd allocated himself probably twice the work he'd assigned her, Ben finished first and he waited while she finished the last little incision and dressed the tiny wound. Then he held the leg in the air away from the guards while she slowly bandaged it, taking care to apply even compression over the entire length.

Several similar operations followed. During the last case, just before five when the list was scheduled to finish, the haematologist who was looking after her own patient, little Rachel Bright with her acute leukaemia, came into theatre to see Ben.

Holding a mask to his face, he peered in. 'Ben, I've got a nineteen-year-old downstairs who turned up this afternoon in A and E. Looks like a T-cell ALL,' he said, referring to a type of acute leukaemia. 'We want to start chemo tonight if we can. I know this isn't the best time but, since he's here, any chance of you slipping in a Hickman for us?' he asked, mentioning the name of the type of intravenous line that Claire had seen in Rachel. 'Ideally before we take him over to our side?' the haematologist ventured.

'Starved?'

'Nothing since nine.'

Ben looked at his anaesthetist, who promptly said, 'I'll run over and assess him.' She asked Molly to call the SHO who was working with Lisa's anaesthetist to come and take over. 'I'm happy to stay to do the case.'

'Molly and Lynn?'

Both woman nodded.

'Thanks, everyone.' The haematologist waved and retreated, and the anaesthetist left with him.

The new patient hadn't arrived from Casualty by the time they finished their last case, and a nurse rang to say there'd be a few minutes' delay while he had an ECG, a tracing of the heart rhythm, which Ben's anaesthetist wanted to see.

Ben headed for the telephone. 'Checking X-ray he realises we need the image intensifier,' he told Claire when she looked at him enquiringly.

Claire nodded. The image intensifier was a machine

that took moving X-ray pictures, enabling the surgeon to check that the line was being inserted correctly.

She went to see if there was anything she could do to help the others, but their patient was awake in Recovery and Lynn had already set up for the Hickman line insertion and she was scrubbing again. Molly wasn't there.

Lisa walked in via the anaesthetic room, wearing the sort of lead-lined over-apron that they'd all have to wear to shield their organs from radiation while the image intensifier was operating. 'I'm helping Ben with the Hickman,' she said curtly. 'He needs someone who knows what she's doing.'

'Oh.' Claire stiffened, awkward, wondering why he hadn't told her that himself. 'OK.'

'No point in you staying.'

Resenting the younger woman's imperiousness, Claire objected. 'I'm interested. I want to stay and watch.'

Lisa's eyes narrowed. 'You'll be in the way.'

'I'll stand in the corner.'

'There aren't enough shields.'

But Molly came to Claire's rescue. 'Here's one, honey,' she announced, the doors swinging wildly behind her ample bottom as she charged into the theatre with two aprons on each arm. 'Lisa, the ward's yelling because you haven't written some letter for your first case. They say he can't go home without it.'

'They can wait.' Lisa still eyed Claire.

'They're in a hurry.'

'They can call my house officer.'

'Ben told me to tell you,' Molly said, lifting her hands to her rounded hips.

Ben's name clearly had a power that Molly lacked because without another word Lisa spun around and left.

'Take no notice,' Molly said briskly, helping Claire on with the heavy apron. 'She's sour today.'

'Does that mean she isn't always?' Claire muttered.

Molly chuckled. 'Sweet as pie when she wants to be,'

she said, confirming what Claire knew already despite never witnessing it herself.

She didn't have to stand aside for the operation because, despite Lisa's scathing comment, there was plenty of room and the screen with its large image could be seen from everywhere in the theatre.

Ben and Lisa, Claire noted, worked well together. The other woman seemed to know what he wanted well before he uttered his quiet commands, her movements were quick and fluent and she had a confidence, Claire realised, that she herself had never possessed. But, then, Lisa had at least five years specialist surgical experience whereas she'd only had six months.

Telling herself that Lisa would flounder in general practice failed to lift her unease, forcing Claire to acknowledge that her real qualms concerned the way Lisa worked so closely with Ben and had nothing to do with her surgical skills.

As they were finishing Lisa was called to the telephone, leaving Ben to lift away the guards and complete the dressing. He looked at Claire standing carefully to the side, his eyes shadowed above the mask. 'Bored?'

'Fascinated,' she countered.

An orderly came in with a trolley and Ben tugged down his mask before helping him to lift their patient from the operating table across onto the trolley. 'Give me a few minutes,' he told Claire. 'I'll finish here and we'll have coffee.'

'Ben, Tony Wilding's looking for you.' Lisa opened the door. 'He's got a renal transplant scheduled for tonight but two more kidneys have become available and they've got possible recipients coming in. He wants to know if we can do one.'

'I'll come and talk to him.' He shrugged at Claire. 'Sorry.'

'I don't mind.' Despite Lisa's triumphant look in her direction she even managed a smile. After she'd

changed, she poked her head back into Theatres in case
he was still there, realising she hadn't thanked him for
the afternoon, but Molly told her that he'd left directly
after speaking to the other surgeon. 'He might be over
at the renal ward,' she said. 'Try calling him there.'

But she didn't want to bother him if he was busy so
she went to visit Angela Dunning, David's patient with
asthma, whom she'd admitted the night before.

Although she was still wheezy Angela looked much
brighter, and her peak flow chart showed a good response to treatment. She was blowing 380 now, whereas
a note at the front of the chart said she'd been unable to
record a reading when first admitted, suggesting she'd
deteriorated quickly after she'd arrived in A and E. 'I
think they put Ventolin into this,' Angela told her, indicating the drip in her left arm. 'I was out of it by then.'

'You're obviously doing much better now,' Claire
said reassuringly. 'Are you still having the nebulisers?'

'Every four hours,' Angela confirmed, 'or sooner if I
need it, but I haven't since lunchtime. They're going to
give me back my inhalers tomorrow and if everything's
all right I'll be able to go home Saturday.'

'I'll let Dr Gibson know,' Claire said. Warren was on
call for the weekend and, given how quickly Angela's
attack had worsened, she suspected David would want
Warren to know that she was being discharged. 'One of
our other doctors might drop in and see you after you
leave.'

Ben got home about eight, by which time she and Jamie
had eaten and Jamie had had his bath and was in his
pyjamas at her feet, watching television while she flicked
through the latest *British Medical Journal*.

Ben stopped by the door, deposited his briefcase and
hugged Jamie when he ran to him. 'I have to go back,'
he said quietly, looking at Claire. 'Surgery's scheduled
for nine-thirty. Any chance of dinner?'

'Roast chicken in the fridge,' she confirmed, dropping the journals on the floor, surprised he'd bothered to come home at all. 'And some salad. If you take Jamie to bed I'll fix the food.'

She felt him come into the kitchen ten minutes later. 'He's OK?'

'Sleepy,' he confirmed.

'Nothing interesting at the canteen?'

'Has there ever been?'

Carefully she turned the remains of the chicken she was carving. 'You eat there so often I assumed it had improved.'

'It's convenient,' he said carefully, 'but I want to reduce the number of hours I spend at the hospital. A lot of my paperwork and reading can be done here and there's no need for me to work late more than a couple of times a week.'

Claire blinked. 'What?'

'Didn't you hear me?'

'I did, but…' She shook her head slightly. 'I'm glad,' she said finally. 'Jamie misses you.'

'Is he the only one?'

'No.' She felt herself blushing and lowered her head quickly to hide that from him. 'I'm glad, too,' she said quietly. 'Tonight, what are you doing? The renal transplants?'

'One of them.' She felt his gaze on her. 'Claire, I'm sorry if Lisa gave you a hard time today. Molly said something about it,' he added quickly in response to her sharp look, 'and I had a word with her. Don't take it personally—she's not happy at the moment. She wants to continue vascular work but there's no post available after September. She's going to have to do something else or change rotations.'

'So she's not staying with you?' she mumbled, tossing the remains of the salad she and Jamie had begun earlier.

'She's not staying with me,' he confirmed.

'Poor Lisa.' Then, remembering the registrar's supercilious manner the night of Duncan Allbright's farewell when they'd discussed just that issue, Claire slapped a drumstick onto his plate. 'No wonder she's suffering. Perhaps I should send her a card?'

'Stop it, Claire.'

But his disapproval rattled her. 'You'll forgive me if I don't weep for the girl,' she stated. 'It's obvious how she feels.'

'Is that important?'

'Of course it's important.' She glared at him. They were talking frankly at last for the first time in a long time, she realised, even if it didn't seem to be bringing them closer. 'Am I supposed to ignore it?'

Ben tilted his head, his eyes assessing. 'I told you about her worries so you'd understand—'

'I understand her well enough.' Claire dumped a splattering of salad onto the plate beside the chicken and shoved it across to him. 'If she'd worn that smock any tighter she'd have burst out of it.'

'Cat.' But she saw that his eyes were glittering now. He left the stool and came around to her. 'You're jealous.'

'Haven't I got a right to be?' she flared.

'You tell me.' He backed her against the sink. 'There are lots of things I could say,' he rasped. 'I could say she's sensitive—'

'Ha!' Claire felt like screaming her frustration that he could be so obtuse. 'As sensitive as a brick,' she snapped.

Ben smiled. He leaned towards her, bracing his arms against the bench so that she was trapped, his mouth at her ear. 'I could say she's confused—'

'Confused? You're mad,' she retorted. 'You know exactly what she wants.'

'Pull your claws in,' he chided softly, moving closer so that she felt him against her. 'Stop interrupting.' One hand shifted to her hip, holding her. 'I could say we're close.'

'That much I guessed,' she hissed. 'You've no shame—'

'And she's vulnerable.' While she stayed locked stiff, with cool Belfast stone against the small of her back, he tilted her backwards, his mouth tracking leisurely across the neck—arousing her powerfully when she didn't want to be aroused.

'And possibly even she cares for me.' His tongue probed a tiny hollow, making her shiver. 'Ring any bells?' he murmured against her skin. 'Hmm? Anything sound familiar to you, Claire?'

'You...' And then she jerked her head and pushed him violently, determined to escape, but he was too strong for her, holding her easily despite her struggles. 'How dare you!' she raged. 'Those things I said about David were genuine. Truthful. And that was completely innocent, you know that. Nothing to do with your sordid little...'

She stopped, the words too painful for her to voice, but he didn't release her.

'My sordid what?' he demanded, his mouth tight now, his eyes harsh where seconds before he had been easy, teasing. 'What, Claire? Tell me.'

'You know,' she whispered.

'Do I?'

'Even if nothing happened, you thought about it,' she said desperately, her voice agonised. 'I could tell. That day. Before Scotland. I could see it in your eyes.'

'And, if I did, would that be so surprising?' Abruptly he released her, let her fall back against the bench. 'Think. Would it?'

'She's beautiful,' she said weakly.

'And you aren't?' Abruptly he turned impatient. 'Look in the mirror sometimes, Claire. Why the hell do you think David's so desperate to get his hands on you?'

'It isn't like that.'

'It is from where I'm standing,' he said harshly. 'Delude yourself if it suits you, but it doesn't work for me.'

'No, Lisa works for you,' she muttered.

Ben swore under his breath. 'Lisa has nothing to do with this,' he said roughly. 'This is you and me, Claire. No one else.'

'If it wasn't for her—'

'Lisa doesn't have anything to do with the hours you've been working,' he retorted. 'Nothing to do with you being so wrapped up and self-satisfied with the wonderful job you're doing at the practice that for two years you've forgotten you've a son and husband who would like more time with you. A son and husband who can't stand to see you exhausted and drained in the few hours you can spare for them.'

His expression darkened. 'Lisa has nothing to do with the fact that you decided we should no longer share a bed. Nothing to do with the fact that until this week you hadn't come to me in ten months, and even then it was only because I picked you up and carried you there and bloody near forced you to stay. Nothing to do with the fact that as soon as I leave for a few hours you scuttle back to your own bed again.'

He stepped back, surveying her shock with something akin to satisfaction. 'Good, Claire,' he said, so softly she had to strain to hear. 'Very good. Now you're starting to realise. I think even the most reasonable of men might have found grounds among all of that for a little…entertainment. Hmm? Beginning to make sense?'

Horrible, awful sense, but still she protested. 'Last night…I thought you'd need your sleep,' she said weakly. 'After going out so late. I thought my being there would stop you from sleeping.'

'I hadn't slept the night before. Did it feel like I minded?'

'No.' She flushed, turned her head away, remembering.

'And that doesn't explain why you changed rooms in the first place.'

'You know why,' she said defensively. 'I explained. It was for you as much as me. I didn't want to disturb you either when I was working but that didn't mean…you still could have come to me.'

'For you to dutifully fulfil your wifely responsibilities?' he asked acidly. 'Hardly, Claire. No man wants that.'

'That isn't how it would have been.'

'That's how it would have felt.'

'Oh.' She wrapped her arms around herself forlornly, wishing she'd realised—then perhaps this could all have been avoided. But she'd been busy, of course, as he'd noted so plainly, and tired—so often tired. The weeks had become months and then, by the time she'd realised what was happening, they'd drifted apart and her confidence had faded to the point where she'd no longer felt able to approach him.

Even tonight, even now that they'd been together again, she realised she probably wouldn't have had the confidence to touch him without him first coming to her.

'So what now?' she whispered.

'You tell me,' he said tightly. 'Obviously we can't go on like this.'

She stared at him, her pulse hammering in her chest, appalled. 'What about Jamie?'

'Jamie…? Ben's mouth twisted. 'You mean divorce?' he demanded harshly. 'Divorce? Is that what you want?'

She could feel herself shrinking, feel her skin creeping in on itself. 'Isn't that what you meant?'

'God, Claire!' He looked as shocked as she felt and for a few seconds they just stood there, staring at each other.

CHAPTER EIGHT

BEN opened his mouth as if to continue, but the chime of his watch broke the contact and he pulled away and swore violently. 'I have to go,' he rasped.

'You haven't eaten.' Frantic now and desperate to keep herself busy, Claire twirled around, trying to remember where she kept the cling film. 'You have to eat,' she said hoarsely. 'You must eat.'

'There's no time.'

'Take it with you.' She found the film in a drawer and tore off a hunk but it stuck to itself, tangled in her shaking fingers and she screwed it up, thrust it away and wrenched more. She wrapped it over the plate, hurrying, but it wasn't enough, left gaps, and so she picked up the plate to wrap it again and again from the roll until the film formed a thick cover over the food.

'Take it,' she repeated, thrusting it at him. 'You might be up all night.'

'I might.' He carried the plate to the door. 'Are you home tomorrow?'

'I'm on call.' She felt breathless. 'Mary's getting Jamie again.'

'I'll collect him after work.' He gave her a hard, unreadable look then left.

She managed to get upstairs, to get all the way through cleansing her face and brushing her teeth and changing into her pyjamas before she started to cry. When she woke in the morning her pillow was still damp.

Ben's unruffled bed told her that he hadn't been home

118

and she schooled her expression as she went to wake Jamie.

Victor and Julie Bright, the couple she'd been seeing for marriage counselling, came as her last scheduled appointment of the day. 'We wanted to thank you,' Julie said happily, her hands entwined with her husband's, 'for everything you've done. We feel we've discovered each other again.'

'The doctors say that it's still early but that Rachel's white blood count is falling exactly the way it should,' Victor said, his face split with a smile that hadn't faded since their arrival. 'They're confident.'

'That's wonderful news.' Claire was aware of Rachel's progress because she'd rung the haematology registrar on the team looking after her that morning for an update, but seeing Victor and Julie's obvious joy refreshed her pleasure.

'Whatever happens,' Julie said softly, 'we'll face it together. We're both stronger that way.'

'It's just taken a long time to realise it,' Victor confirmed.

Wondering anew at the irony of her helping this couple to become closer while her own marriage seemed hell-bent on deteriorating, Claire managed to stay smiling as she showed them out.

David was at Reception and he looked up when she came out. 'Success?' he enquired, when the couple had left.

'For a change,' she said, noting the empty waiting-room and hoping that boded well for the evening clinic scheduled to start in thirty minutes. 'A quiet night would be bliss.'

But her comment seemed to have pricked either David's curiosity or his sympathy because he followed her back to her office. 'Bad day?'

'No, not really,' she said hurriedly, leaning against the

frame of her door. 'Oh, it's Friday. Almost holiday time for you. Looking forward to it?'

'Not particularly.' He lifted one shoulder almost uncertainly, his pale gaze moving about her room. 'There are some things I'll miss around here.'

Before she'd decided whether it was wise to ask more, Warren's door opened and he hurtled out with a speed that belied his size. 'No work?' he said sharply, his eyes darting between them. 'Want some of mine?'

'No, thanks.' Claire smiled at him. 'Believe it or not, I treasure my quiet hours.'

'What about you, David?' Warren peered at him. 'Time to be getting away, isn't it? Thought you'd be gone already.'

'Did you?' David didn't shift. 'Actually, I wanted to talk to Claire,' he said defensively, sounding to Claire rather like a schoolboy confronting his headmaster.

But, to Claire's surprise, instead of withdrawing, Warren said crisply, 'You're busy, aren't you, Claire?'

'Not especially,' she said slowly, not understanding what was going on. 'I can't leave because of evening clinic.'

David glared at Warren, before looking back at her. 'Then we can talk.'

But when he stepped towards her Warren put his arm out. 'I need your antenatal figures,' the older man said. 'I'm ready to put the claims in.'

'I'll do them later,' David snapped. 'Before I leave.'

'I need them now.'

'Warren...?'

'David.' Warren's face was stiff and Claire stared at them both in disbelief. She'd never heard them talk like this. They disagreed occasionally but now she sensed real antagonism between them.

'You're behaving unreasonably,' David protested. 'There's no urgency for those figures.'

'It won't take you long. Less than ten minutes.'

'All right.' David backed out, his face strained, sparing Claire a brief, oddly imploring look before he went to his office.

As soon as his door had closed Warren turned back to her. 'Now, Claire,' he said carefully, making her stiffen as she wondered if she was in for the same sort of treatment. But Warren merely told her that Susan Drury had called earlier to ask for a repeat prescription of her lithium to be ready for the following Monday. 'Actually, I don't believe she sounded very well,' he mused.

Claire straightened. 'Depressed?'

'Perhaps.' He peered at her. 'She did say she'd be home this afternoon. Given how brittle that young lady can be, perhaps it would be a good idea..?'

'I'll run around and see her,' Claire said quickly, agreeing with his concern. Knowing how ill Susan could get, she was determined to keep a close eye on her, particularly during this immediate post-discharge period when she'd be especially vulnerable to relapse. 'There's time before clinic.'

'Oh, I can see anyone who turns up,' Warren said benignly. 'No hurry.'

'Thank you.' But she gave him a vaguely doubtful look, puzzled that he'd hurried David so urgently yet now seemed quite calm.

Susan admitted that she was a little upset about not having found a job but assured Claire that she wasn't feeling depressed. 'It's only been two weeks,' she said calmly. 'My benefit's enough to survive on for a little while longer.'

Claire noted that the living-room and kitchen sparkled and that the windows had been cleaned since the last time she'd visited.

'Me,' Susan admitted wryly when Claire questioned her. 'When I'm bored I clean. I'm driving the others mad.' Then she laughed. 'Well, madder, I suppose I should say,' she added, 'considering they're all ex-St Paul's patients.'

Claire smiled, eyeing the younger woman thoughtfully. She'd had two more faxed résumés from the agency she'd approached, but one of the applicants spoke little English and the other was studying it but didn't sound as if she spoke it well enough to help Jamie with his schoolwork. She'd also flatly refused to consider housework, regardless of how much extra money it earned her.

A few minutes later it was settled and Susan seemed delighted, agreeing to take the job at least until something else came up. 'If I stay well for long enough I might decide to try university again,' she warned.

But Claire was happy just to have her now, and beyond that she was pleased that Susan had regained the confidence to even contemplate returning to study.

There would be a month's trial, they decided, during which time Susan would remain at the halfway house so that she retained the support of the friends she'd made there. 'You can use the Fiat,' Claire told her, referring to the small car which had once belonged to her but now was used by the nannies for things like shopping and for collecting Jamie from school. 'After the month, if it works out and you're happy, you're welcome to come and live with us,' she continued, stiffening as she forced away the thought that 'us' might mean just her and Jamie by then. They agreed that Susan would come around on Sunday evening to meet Jamie and see the house.

Susan's smile showed relief, and Claire suspected that she'd been more worried about finding work than she'd let on. 'I can't thank you enough, Dr Marshall.'

'Claire,' Claire said firmly. 'And this is not altruistic, Susan. I need your help.'

Warren's car was the lone one in the car park when she arrived back at the surgery, and the absence of any patients in the waiting-room signalled what turned out to be a quiet evening. She stayed until eight-thirty, mainly doing paperwork, because the only two people who came to the clinic simply wanted repeat prescriptions and she discovered both, already signed by David, waiting at the desk.

Ben's Saab was in the garage and lights were on in the living-room and kitchen but she found them upstairs, Ben reading to Jamie from an old favourite, A.A. Milne's *When we were very young* book of rhymes. Ben sat facing away from the door so she exchanged a secret smile with Jamie before going to change, leaving James James Morrison Morrison to Ben.

When she emerged from her room Ben had gone downstairs. She sat on Jamie's bed and they talked about his win in his class's swimming competition and about a new computer game his friend, Mitch, had been given.

'Prawn salad in the fridge, if you're hungry.' Ben looked up from his *Lancet* when she finally ventured into the living-room, his expression unreadable. 'Many calls?'

'It's quiet.' She heard nervousness in her voice and hoped it wasn't as obvious to him. 'How did the transplant go last night?'

'Uneventful. Our recipient's doing well.'

'I'm glad.'

'Are you?'

'Of course.' Flustered now, her tenseness increased and, suddenly clumsy, she managed to catch her leg painfully against the edge of the door as she turned away, prompting an involuntary gasp that drew a mildly concerned look from Ben.

Had he thought more about the things he'd said last night? she fretted, her heart hammering, as she limped to the kitchen. Had he come to any decisions?

She had no appetite but, deciding that she ought to eat, she forced herself to dish out a little of the leftover salad she assumed he'd bought from the supermarket earlier that evening.

'I opened a bottle of wine,' Ben said, coming into the room in time, she suspected, to catch her wince as she hauled herself up onto one of the breakfast-bar stools and managed to bump her sore shin again in the process. He opened the fridge. 'Want a glass?'

'I'm on call.'

'A few mouthfuls won't hurt,' he said coolly, pouring the wine despite her protest. 'It'll calm your nerves.'

'There's nothing wrong with my nerves,' she declared, ignoring his raised eyebrows when she dropped her fork for the second time since he'd come into the room.

'You're not normally butter-fingered.'

'It's not a normal evening.' She studied one perfect pink prawn, then replaced her fork and pushed her plate away. From past occasions she knew that the salad was delicious, but she'd been wrong to think she could eat when she felt like this. 'I don't know what to say to you.'

'Because of last night?'

'You said you wanted a divorce.'

'I said things couldn't continue the way they'd been going,' he countered coolly. 'You said divorce.'

'Because it was obviously what you meant.' She looked up, her voice rising. 'Was I supposed to wait submissively like a good little wife until you decided to bring it up yourself?' While, in the meantime, the unspoken threat would have hung over her like a guillotine?

The corners of his mouth tightened. 'Do you really think that?'

'I don't know what to think.' She could hear the anguish she was too distraught to try and disguise. 'I can't read you now, after all these years, any more than I ever could. My head's going in circles. I can't think properly about anything.' She took a hasty sip of the drink he'd passed her, then pushed that away, too. 'What do you want? Please, no games, just tell me what you want and let me deal with it.'

'I told you after Scotland that I wasn't leaving.'

'People change their minds.'

'And Jamie?'

Her face froze. 'Stays with me,' she said jerkily.

'What about David?'

'Stop it.' She surged off her stool, the pain in her leg now faint compared with her distress. 'There's nothing between David and me. You're only implying there is to try and distract attention from Lisa.'

The air between them thickened and she sensed his anger. 'Would I take you to work with me if I was having an affair with her?' he demanded, the coldness of his words at variance with the heat she could see glowing behind his eyes. 'Am I that disturbed in your eyes, Claire, that I'd do something like that?'

'Perhaps it's over,' she whispered, backing away. 'Over between the two of you. Perhaps you don't want her any more. Perhaps you took me there to force her to see that.'

'If that's the case, you've nothing to worry about,' he said icily. 'Clearly if I've sacrificed my mistress it's because I don't plan to leave my wife.'

'You mean you don't want to leave your son.' When his mouth clamped shut, when he said nothing to dispute that, she turned away bitterly, her arms crossed over her body as she stared out into the garden. 'What are you saying?'

'No divorce. Not now.'

'And later?'

'I'll never let you go to David,' he growled. 'If you try and take Jamie to him—'

'David means nothing to me,' she said harshly, her voice shaking, spinning to confront his shuttered face—barely believing that Ben still dwelt on something so unimportant when there was so much else at stake. 'He's my friend, that's all. He's been hurt—'

'He's weak.' Ben's face bore no compassion, no understanding—only bitter condemnation. 'And stupid as hell if he thought I'd let you go so easily. You're mine, Claire. Whatever happens, I won't let you go to him.'

Whatever happens. She shivered at the fierce possessiveness of the words and of the gaze that raked her. 'I'm not a toy,' she protested, so faintly that she knew her words were barely audible. 'I'm not something you fight over in the playground.'

His eyes darkened. 'I'm not playing, Claire.'

'David is one of my partners,' she said wearily.

'He wants more than that.'

'You're wrong. He's just not himself at the moment. He's been under a lot of strain. He told me…the next day he told me he hadn't meant the things he'd said.'

'He can't keep away from you.'

'That's not true.' And it wasn't, either, not that Ben would know one way or the other. 'I've hardly seen him. And he's on holiday now for two weeks. He's going away.'

Ben folded his arms and leaned back against the bench, his expression speculative. 'Not a good working environment for marriages,' he said coolly. 'Your little surgery. Warren, Martin, David, all living without their wives.'

'Medical marriages,' she said warily, unsure where he was heading now. 'Statistically high risk of failure. You must see it yourself among your colleagues.'

'Not like that.'

'And we can hardly hold ourselves up as a blazing success story.' She uncrossed her arms, stiff from hugging herself. 'Considering.'

'You need another partner. Another partner would

ease the stress on all of you. If you'd accepted one earlier, Martin and David might still have their wives.'

'That's ridiculous. David's talked about what went wrong and it was nothing to do with work.'

'Rebecca told me two years ago that she wanted out.'

Claire's head snapped up. David had professed not to have known there was any problem with their relationship until Rebecca had walked out on him.

'They hardly saw each other,' he continued. 'She'd warned him—begged him to ask you all about taking on an extra GP.'

'Rebecca left him for another man,' she said hoarsely.

'David's rationalisation,' he said harshly. 'God knows, he's got enough of them. She'd been miserable for years. She'd been living virtually alone throughout their entire marriage.'

'It was adultery.'

'Brought on by neglect.'

'She had a lover.'

'Who can blame her?'

'Not you,' she said acidly. 'Obviously.'

But he didn't flinch, didn't look remotely shamed. 'We've been through this.'

And she'd been through it a hundred times in her head since, she acknowledged. And nothing had changed. 'When did you talk to Rebecca?'

Ben's face closed. 'We spoke several times.'

'When?'

'When makes no difference,' he said coldly. 'She was looking for support. She wanted help to convince you all that your hours were unreasonable. She wanted to know if it was the same with you—if I saw as little of you as she did of her husband.'

'And what did you tell her?'

'That I'd do my best.'

'You didn't say anything.'

'I've tried to get you to take on someone,' he said

grimly, 'but neither you nor Warren will admit you're overworked.'

'My hours are less than yours.'

'I cope,' he declared. 'You barely get by and the others lost their marriages.'

'We do a good job.'

'I'm not arguing with that.'

No. He wasn't. But he was arguing about her work, she realised. *Her* work. Always, whatever way they started, always, at some stage with him, it came back to that. 'You can't blame my work this time,' she cried. 'It's not my job that's destroying us, it's you. You and what you've done with Lisa. That's what's done the harm—'

'I haven't touched her,' he roared.

Claire felt the colour drain out of her face.

'I won't deny she's willing,' he added harshly, 'but that's not the same.'

She gaped. 'But...Scotland?'

'She was there to tutor. She might have had other ideas. I didn't.'

Claire sank onto the low-level window ledge behind her, rubbing absently at the still throbbing calf she'd injured earlier. 'Why didn't you tell me?'

'Why didn't you trust me?'

'Because...' She stopped, unsure exactly when the trust had gone. When Jamie had mentioned her? When David had seen them having dinner together, perhaps? 'That night when you brought her here I asked you. I would have believed you then, but you didn't deny anything.'

'I was angry that I had to.'

'I thought...' She shook her head slowly. 'I assumed—'

'Wrongly.'

'But yesterday...She doesn't act like it's just a working relationship.'

With one lift of a broad shoulder he dismissed Lisa's possessiveness as inconsequential. 'I'm her supervisor,' he said indifferently. 'She finds a certain…appeal in that which has nothing to do with me personally. It isn't the first time something like that's happened and it won't be the last. You were the same once.'

Claire flushed hotly, remembering. Only it hadn't been his role as her supervisor which had attracted her but him, Ben himself. Physically, of course, he'd been powerfully appealing, but for her the attraction had quickly grown deeper than that. At work she'd been moved by his dedication and his compassion and the way they'd connected intellectually and emotionally. She'd never considered hiding her adoration. 'With me you didn't say no,' she said faintly.

'I didn't even try.'

Their eyes met and the glitter in his told her he recalled that first time as vividly as she. She'd been working for him for only two weeks but already he'd aroused feelings in her that had left her restless and disturbed—acutely disturbed—given that she'd assumed her priority in life to be her career.

She'd been innocent physically but that hadn't dulled the intensity of her desire, nor had it made him grant any concessions, although her virginity must have been blindingly obvious to him.

The first time they'd made love had been in his office, a small, cramped, overheated room with a jammed-on radiator where they'd gone for coffee after a long session together in the operating theatre. He'd saved a patient's leg, she remembered, a butcher who'd accidentally plunged his knife into his groin while splitting a carcass. Ben had stemmed the bleeding and repaired the severed femoral artery which would otherwise have proved fatal.

They'd been drinking coffee, that was all at first, but the hours working beside him had aroused her, left her dreamy and bemused, and she hadn't been able to take her eyes off him.

Without warning he'd bent forward and kissed her and although she'd gasped her shock it had been shock mingled with delight—delight which had thickened into tense desire when he'd kicked the door shut, carelessly swept papers and books to the floor, lifted her onto his desk and parted her clothes.

Even that first time, with no bed, no comfort, his bleeper liable to shrill at any time and the room so hot they'd both been damp with sweat before he'd even touched her, it had been urgent and passionate and mindlessly pleasurable.

Later in his flat and again wherever they'd found they could be together the gloriousness had never dimmed for her. She found herself madly and wildly in love with him and deliriously happy.

Very close to the end of her six-month attachment she'd discovered she was pregnant, a result of one of many occasions when their passions had overcome their access to prevention. At first she hadn't been concerned when her period hadn't come—as a doctor, she'd been confident about the pattern of her cycle and she'd thought they'd been safe. But she'd been wrong.

Ben, though, hadn't been dismayed and his pleasure and immediate proposal had filled her with joy.

After her attachment finished she'd gone to work at the practice where she worked now. At the time it had seemed the easiest path for her to follow—in those days surgery was too competitive to allow for part-time training around childbearing.

They'd married quickly, a small, perfect wedding, followed by a brief but idyllic honeymoon in the Maldives where they'd done little except explore the warm waters and each other. Then Jamie's arrival had made what she'd thought was a perfect existence—sublime—and at

the time she'd envisaged a future full of joy and fulfilment.

But she'd been naïve, she realised. And quite wrong.
They'd lost completely the thoughtless happiness of
those early years. And things were getting worse.

She met Ben's dark gaze hesitantly. 'I loved you,' she
whispered. 'It wasn't the power thing you're implying.'

'It was at first.'

'No.' She was sure of that. 'No, not at first. Not ever.'

'Remember my office?'

'Yes.' She felt weak. 'Ben…?'

'Remember what we did?'

'Yes.'

'Like this.' He picked her up, spun her around, lifted
her onto the granite and pushed away the plate with her
untouched food. 'It was good, wasn't it?'

'Yes.' She let her head fall back, let him unfasten her
clothing, her breath coming too fast to say more.

He undressed, pulled her into him, came towards her.
'Remember the heat?'

'Yes.' As if they were there again, she could. Dry,
cloying, year-round heat which had blasted from the hospital's radiators. Her eyes closed involuntarily and she
caught her lower lip between her teeth as she felt him
hard against her. 'The coffee.'

'It spilled,' he confirmed, his hands under her thighs,
lifting her onto him. 'Coffee everywhere. In your
clothes, through your hair, against your skin. Remember?'

He moved inside her and she gasped, her fingers curling into his powerful shoulders. 'I didn't care.'

'Like this.' Thrusting into her, slowly, maddeningly,
his hand at her half-bared breast pushed her flat. 'Hmm?'

'Yes.' She arched, ached, shifted, and seconds later
his mouth on hers captured her cry.

But afterwards, when he withdrew and when she finally found the strength to lift eyelids which had grown

terribly heavy, she felt sick. The intimacy their memories and that act had roused was fake. It had evaporated as fast as their fulfilment. What they had now was sex. Not pure sex, but the ashes of a past passion which had once been bathed in love but which now fulfilled the body without replenishing the soul. Sex was where they could reach each other. But sex wasn't a solution to their problems.

'I'm sorry,' she said slowly, bracing herself on her elbows and then managing to sit up. 'About Lisa. I let myself doubt…I was wrong not to trust you.'

His clothes were now fastened, and he looked at her with a brooding remoteness that made her shiver, although she could still see the fading stain of their passion dulling his cheeks. 'We've both made mistakes,' he conceded quietly, watching impassively as she buttoned her blouse. 'Lately, just more of them.'

Her fingers stilled. 'What can I do?'

'What do you want to achieve?'

'I want us to be good parents to Jamie.'

'Speak to Warren. Talk about taking on another partner. Reduce your hours.'

'Does it really just come down to that?' she asked faintly.

'It's a start.' His certainty warned her he'd make no concessions. 'It's not just the hours you spend away but how you are when you're home. Jamie deserves more than a token mother.'

'And you?'

'I want more than a token wife.'

'Do my feelings count?'

'Will your work seem any less satisfying at forty hours than it does at ninety?'

'If I don't do this,' she said slowly, ignoring his question—tilting her head, determined to catch every minute change in his expression. 'If I don't do these things that you demand, what will happen?'

'I can't answer that, Claire.' His face was cold now. Hard. He stooped to gather a tea-towel which must have fallen to the floor when they'd been making love.

'And if I do? If I give in, will everything be back the way it was?'

He stilled. 'You see reducing your workload as giving in to me?'

'It's what you want.'

'I want it for you.'

'You want it so your life becomes smooth again—controlled,' she countered. 'So there are no more crises. So you can stop worrying I'll ask you to do something that might unsettle your routine.'

For a few seconds they just stared at each other, his stare hard and closed, hers, she knew, angry and defensive. If it weren't for the moistness between her thighs, she realised, she wouldn't have been able to believe that they'd been together so passionately only minutes before.

'It's your decision,' he said, and his coolness turned her pale.

CHAPTER NINE

BEN went upstairs to his study, leaving Claire chilled and shaken. Finally an ultimatum, she realised sickly, gripping the edge of the bench for support. Him or her work.

Inwardly she knew she had no choice but some part of her still fought his ruthlessness and bitterly resented the power he wielded so effortlessly. If she only had herself to think of, something inside her argued defiantly, she might have resisted. But she sagged and lowered her head to her clenched hands, acknowledging that in truth she probably wouldn't have.

She slept in her own bed and he didn't disturb her.

In the morning a note in the kitchen informed her he'd gone to the hospital, and she left for the Saturday clinic she was scheduled to cover as soon as her mother arrived to mind Jamie.

Her last patient of the morning, a seventy-year-old man, hobbled into the surgery just before the clinic was due to finish. Pale-faced and obviously in pain, he walked jerkily to a chair, nodding brief appreciation when she rushed to help him. 'Back giving me trouble,' he rasped, one hand going to his left flank. 'Overdid the digging in the garden yesterday. Been bad all night and this morning. Couldn't do the lawn today so I thought I better come in and get something to loosen up these old bones.'

Claire kept one hand on his wrist, checking his pulse while she briefly scanned the notes the receptionist had retrieved. 'No back problems in the past, Mr Coakes?'

'The odd ache,' he admitted. 'Nothing like this.'

She skimmed through Warren's notes, noting that the patient had been taking blood-pressure medication for ten years, with reasonable, although not perfect control whenever Warren had checked his pressures. 'No heart problems?' she asked, wrapping a cuff around his upper arm. 'Angina? Shortness of breath? Swollen ankles?'

'Nothing,' he gasped, sitting forward awkwardly to grip the area around his left hip. 'It's coming on now.'

Quickly she pumped up the cuff, then snapped the arms of her stethoscope into her ears and lowered the pressure slowly, listening at his brachial artery. Frowning, she rechecked the pressures, worried at the uncharacteristic reading. One-ten over seventy was low for someone whose last two readings had been above 160/90. 'You're still taking the same medication?' she asked.

'No change in years.'

His contorted expression eased slightly and Claire said sharply, 'The pain's coming and going?'

'A bit.'

He was still sitting forward, and through his shirt she ran her hand firmly down the centre of his spine. 'Pain here?'

'Off to the side.' He bent his head towards the left.

'Here?' She probed the area around his left kidney.

'Not now.' He shook his head weakly.

She pressed a sticky thermometer to his forehead. 'Noticed any blood in your urine? Any fevers? Hot and cold shakes?' When he shook his head to her questions she continued, 'Any chest pain? Faintness?'

He shook his head again and after waiting a few moments for his temperature to register she noted that it was normal, then said, 'You've never had kidney stones?'

'My wife did,' he told her, and she remembered from the notes that he was recently widowed. 'Years ago. But never me.' Then he frowned. 'This is just the sort of pain she got then. Could it be stones, Doctor? Rather than my back?'

'I can't be sure,' she admitted. But it would be reassuring to find blood in his urine, a common finding with kidney stones, and she went to fetch Leslie, the practice nurse on duty for the morning.

'I can manage,' he told her when together they helped him to the bathroom and so they shut the door and waited outside.

As soon as he emerged Leslie took the sample he'd produced for testing and a short time later she poked her head around the door and said, 'Clear of everything. No glucose, no protein, no blood.'

'Thanks.' By now Claire had Mr Coakes on her examination couch and, after checking that the neurological function in his lower limbs was intact—wanting to exclude a spinal disc injury from her short-list—she turned her attention to his abdomen. First she checked that the pulses in his groin were normal, before probing gently and carefully. When her fingers encountered a large, deep mass that moved with the pulsation of his heart she stiffened. 'Mr Coakes, I'm afraid you're going to have to go up to the hospital,' she said quietly, keeping her voice deliberately calm and reassuring. 'There's a swollen blood vessel in your tummy which might be causing your pain but only a specialist at the hospital can tell for sure.'

'I'll get a cab,' he said weakly, lifting his head. 'Don't go to any bother.'

'It's no bother.' She pushed gently against his forehead forcing him to lower his head onto the pillow. 'Relax for a few minutes while I call an ambulance,' she ordered.

She slipped out from behind the curtains, then rushed into David's office to make the calls so that her referral wouldn't alarm her patient. She called the ambulance service, requesting an urgent pick-up and explaining the possible diagnosis.

'Doctor, we've all our blue light crews in action,' the controller said crisply. 'Are you able to go with the patient?'

Since Warren was on call for the weekend, and officially he was covering the practice from now so she was free to leave, Claire confirmed that she could.

'Then eight minutes,' the controller answered. 'I'll divert a unit now.'

Claire rang the hospital. Deciding that this was too urgent for her to waste time playing political games with Lisa, she asked the operator to bleep Ben directly.

He replied quickly, and after explaining that her call was work-related she said, 'Possible dissecting aortic aneurysm,' referring to the process where the swollen artery begins to tear, a process which could lead to complete and—without emergency surgery—fatal rupture. She rushed through her findings. 'The artery feels about six centimetres wide but I didn't risk probing too much. The ambulance is on its way.'

'Good heath otherwise?'

'Hypertension, otherwise excellent health.'

'Send him straight in,' he said tightly. 'Claire, better put a decent line in. Saline's fine, whatever you've got, just so that there's something there in case the aorta tears through in transit.'

'Straight away.' Claire lowered the receiver and hurried back to her patient. 'I'm going to pop a needle into your arm,' she said calmly, swabbing his forearm after she'd applied a tourniquet. She selected a grey Venflon, not as wide as ones she'd used in hospitals but the largest that they kept at the surgery, and to her relief, because she was out of practice, it inserted smoothly into the vein she'd selected.

She taped the cannula into place, then tugged the blue plastic cover from the nozzle of a 500ml bag of normal saline—the biggest they kept—and inserted the probe of a giving set into the bag, running the fluid through before swapping the needle still in his arm for the tubing.

'Is that my ambulance?' Mr Coakes asked weakly.

'Sounds like it's coming now,' she confirmed, holding his hand. 'How's the pain?'

'Not too bad.' But his grimace warned her of his stoicism. 'Will I need an operation?'

'I think so.' She squeezed his hand. 'Want me to call anyone for you?'

'There isn't anyone,' he said. 'Only the cat.'

'Is there someone who can feed her?'

'My neighbour.' He gave her the number and she copied it onto the top corner of his file. 'If you would let her know, Doctor. That's very kind.'

She sat in the back of the ambulance, belting herself into a seat beside Mr Coakes's stretcher for the short, fast journey to the hospital.

Ben and Lisa were waiting in the emergency department but although the younger woman's delicate eyebrows arched at Claire when she saw her, accompanying her patient, she made no comment.

Nurses, an anaesthetist and Lisa and Ben descended on him while Claire stood to one side, taking care not to get in the way. 'Crossmatch six, let them know we'll probably need more, standard bloods and straight to X-ray,' Ben said quickly to Lisa, after laying a hand on Mr Coakes's abdomen. He exchanged a meaningful look with the anaesthetist, who promptly bent his head to examine their patient's chest.

'It's a big operation,' Ben said solemnly, clasping the older man's hand, 'and I can't make any guarantees. Are you up to it?'

'I'll do my best,' Mr Coakes said faintly. He stared up at Ben. 'We've met before,' he added. 'My wife. Five years ago. She had a blockage in her leg and you fixed her up.' He jumped slightly as Lisa inserted another line, then continued, 'Did a good job, too. She was back in the garden in two weeks—not a bit of trouble afterwards. Not till the heart attack, that is.'

'Lily Coakes?' Claire saw Ben's nod of remembrance. 'Lovely roses, I remember. Old-fashioned ones she'd nurtured herself. She used to bring them to my clinic—most beautiful flowers I've ever seen.'

'That's Lily.' Mr Coakes shook his hand again, seeming pleased that Ben remembered his wife.

'I was sorry to hear she died,' Ben said. 'I read the announcement in the paper.'

'I got your card,' Mr Coakes said, surprising Claire, who hadn't known anything about it. 'You were very kind.'

'She was a lovely woman.' Ben patted his shoulder. 'You must miss her very much.'

'Life's not been the same,' he said sadly. 'But I'm not ready to give up yet,' he said, more strongly now as he stared up at Ben. 'There's the cat and the garden waiting for me. Do your best, son. I can't ask more than that.'

'Some X-rays and a scan first,' Ben said quietly. He lifted his head and nodded for the porters who were poised over Mr Coakes waiting to wheel him away. 'I'll come through with you. Once I see the pictures I'll be able to explain where we go from here.'

Things moved quickly. Claire went with Ben to X-ray, where a radiology registrar immediately confirmed their suspected diagnosis.

'Pressure on the ureter's caused the loin pain,' Ben explained, pointing to where the aneurysm brushed the tube from the kidney on the ultrasound pictures. He looked briefly at Claire. 'Good diagnosis.'

'It wasn't difficult,' she said faintly, but he wasn't listening.

He was already on the phone to Theatre, telling them they were on their way. 'Lisa, go up and scrub,' he ordered. 'I'll go with Mr Coakes.' His house officer was taking more details from Mr Coakes and Ben nodded for him to continue. 'Claire, I'll call you later,' Ben said, as he moved briskly with the trolley towards the exit. 'This might take a few hours.'

Or it might be over quickly, Claire added silently, reading the warning in his expression. She nodded private acknowledgement of his unspoken words and stood back to let them go ahead, feeling strained.

She'd have liked to have gone with them, she realised. General practice was satisfying in that she looked after her patients for many years, unlike in hospital practice where contact was often brief, but, still, sometimes she missed the urgent adrenaline-like rush of surgery. She missed not being able to be there with her patient right through his treatment.

Jamie and her mother were out when she got home, a note on the kitchen bench saying that they'd gone to the river to feed the ducks. She called Mr Coakes's neighbour to explain that he was in hospital and to ask her to feed the cat, which she said she'd be pleased to do, then she rang Warren to let him know what had happened to his patient.

Warren sounded shaken by the news. 'I can't remember the last time I examined his abdomen,' he said roughly. 'When I diagnosed his hypertension, of course, but probably not since. That aneurysm might have been growing for years.'

'He's had no symptoms,' she said reasonably, but she understood how he felt. No matter how hard and how thoroughly they worked, the normal reaction to missing something was always guilt. 'He only came in today because he couldn't do what he wanted in the garden.'

'Who's doing the surgery?'

'Ben.'

'Then he's in the best hands.' Warren sighed. 'And at least they're doing him. I heard they were only doing repairs for patients under sixty-five these days and Mr

Coakes must be at least seventy. Ask Ben to call me later if he gets a chance, Claire. Thanks for letting me know. Have a good weekend.'

'You, too.' But Claire frowned as she hung up, the worry in Warren's voice telling her that he wouldn't forgive himself for not finding the problem earlier.

Her mother and Jamie came home before lunch and they ate sandwiches outside in the warm afternoon sun before her mother went off to play golf.

Ben telephoned around four. 'He's through,' he told her briskly, 'although he'll be in Intensive Care a few days at least. The aneurysm involved the renal arteries, which is why we took so long to finish, but thankfully he's starting to produce some urine.'

She smiled her relief but before she could ask him to call Warren he said that her partner had already been up to see Mr Coakes and that they'd talked. 'Sounds like he's always been a stalwart chap,' he said, referring to Mr Coakes, and dismissing Warren's apparent concern that his aneurysm might have been growing undetected for years. 'His wife was the same.'

'I didn't know you knew her,' she said, remembering Mr Coakes's comment about the card Ben had sent when she'd died, but he sounded as if he was in a hurry so she didn't question him further. 'Are you busy?'

'Fairly,' he said briskly. 'Things have banked up and I'm trying to finish writing up a paper. I'll be late so don't keep dinner.'

'Bye.' She lowered the receiver quietly then lingered a few seconds, before returning to the garden and Jamie.

She didn't see Ben again until late Sunday, long after Susan had visited and met Jamie and left again.

Despite his long hours of duty he didn't look especially tired, although the faint lines around his mouth might have been more pronounced than normal.

'There's coffee made,' she said quietly, following him to the kitchen after his initial greeting.

'Too hot tonight.' He opened the fridge and extracted a cold lager of the low-alcohol type he kept for when he was on call, and had it half-drained in a few long swallows. He lowered the bottle, his eyes coolly assessing as they scanned the brief shorts and T-shirt she still wore. 'Good day?'

'We went swimming,' she told him. It had been an exceptionally warm day and she'd taken Jamie to the pool at Hounslow. 'The lessons have paid off—he's very good. I can see why he's doing so well in the competition at school. How's Mr Coakes?'

'Stable.' He finished the beer, then rinsed and dumped the bottle into the bin in the pantry where they stored bottles for recycling. 'You did well with that. It was only the clot holding the aorta together. Much longer and it would have ruptured completely.'

'Warren said something about the hospital no longer undertaking repairs for patients over sixty-five,' she said.

'That's an administrative recommendation.' Ben's grim expression told her how he felt about administrators making clinical decisions. 'In emergencies like today's it's up to the duty surgeon's discretion. He's a fit and active man. It wouldn't have made sense not to operate.'

'Thank you.'

Ben lifted one shoulder dismissively. 'For doing my job?'

'For doing it so well,' she said quietly.

'We all do our best,' he replied carelessly, taking another drink, a cola this time, and ripping back the tab as he strode towards the door. 'Jamie asleep?'

'He was before.' She went upstairs with him and waited at Jamie's door while he bent to ruffle his sleeping head gently. 'I've found a child-minder,' she said softly, watching Jamie affectionately as she explained about Susan. 'Probably only for a few months, though. She's thinking about going back to university.'

Ben finished his cola. 'Is she happy to help with his schoolwork?'

'We're going to see his teacher one day this week if I can get away early,' Claire confirmed. 'You don't mind about her being one of my patients?' she asked, meaning particularly one of her psychiatric patients.

'You wouldn't have employed her if you had doubts,' he said softly. They backed out of Jamie's room and Ben pulled the door quietly shut. 'How did she and Jamie get on?'

'Well.'

'Good.' Ben watched her. 'It's late,' he said quietly. 'Bed?'

Her face heated. 'About my work,' she said huskily, shifting her weight awkwardly from foot to foot. 'My hours. What we talked about on Friday. I've thought about what you said, but I haven't decided what I'm going to do.'

'It's your decision,' he said, taking her face between his warm hands and bending towards her. 'But leave it for now.' It was a light, gentle, almost experimental kiss, flavoured with the soft drink he'd just finished, but it melted her and she lifted herself against him.

He fell asleep immediately after they'd made love, his breathing calm and regular as he slept heavily in her arms until eventually she drifted into sleep herself.

She woke to a kiss at her cheek but when she turned to embrace Ben, as she'd thought, Jamie's giggles startled her. She jerked, hauling the sheet up to cover her breasts, but, rather than being beside her, Ben was at the doorway, fully dressed in a dark suit and pale shirt and tie.

She flushed as her eyes met his knowing regard briefly before alighting on her laughing son and his gift of orange juice and cereal and coffee in bed for her.

'I made it, Mummy,' Jamie told her, jumping onto the bed, his beam confirming his clear delight at having found her in Ben's bed. 'Daddy helped. He did the coffee and he carried the tray upstairs. Look!' He held up a ragged yellow rose. 'I picked it for you. Do you like it?'

'Of course I do, darling.' She struggled up fully and tucked the sheet around her, her flush deepening as she saw the clothes Ben had carelessly stripped from her the night before strewn around the room. She hugged Jamie. 'What a lovely surprise. Thank you.'

'Are you sleeping in Daddy's bedroom again, Mummy?'

'Er...?' She looked appealingly at Ben but he didn't make any attempt to rescue her, merely studying her in that cool, thoughtful way he had perfected. 'Sometimes,' she said faintly. 'Sometimes Daddy and Mummy have to work at night and that makes it difficult for the one who's trying to sleep.'

'Oh.' But Jamie nodded, seeming to decide that that made sense. 'Susan's coming today,' he announced. 'She's going to look after me. We're going to play soldiers.'

'She'll pick you up from school,' Claire confirmed, pleased that he was looking forward to it. 'I'm going to call your teacher so she knows.'

'I'm late.' Ben came forward, bracing his hands either side of her so that they dug into the mattress when he bent and kissed her. 'Bye, Mummy,' he purred, with a mockery that told her he'd noticed how flustered she was. 'See you tonight.'

'I'm on call,' she said quickly, biting her lower lip when the words cooled his expression, 'but you don't have to rush home. Susan said she's happy to stay until you finish work.'

'I shouldn't be late.' He kissed Jamie. 'Make sure Mummy eats her breakfast,' he instructed, his eyes briefly catching hers again. 'No one can work properly on an empty stomach and Mummy worked hard last night.'

'OK, Daddy.' Jamie's expression set sternly, and from the way he settled himself beside her and folded his arms she saw that he was going to take his orders seriously.

Still flushing from Ben's reference to the night before and acknowledging that he'd manipulated them both, Claire applied herself resignedly to the food.

When she finally got around to seeing Warren that afternoon he was still fretting about missing Mr Coakes's aneurysm. 'Warren, you're a competent and thorough GP,' she told him, not surprised that he still worried because it was exactly how she'd have felt herself. 'And, from what Ben said, even if you'd noticed it months ago the protocols laid down by the administration wouldn't have let him operate, given Mr Coakes's age, anyway. Presenting as an emergency out of hours probably means we've saved his life.'

'Still, I can't help but wonder.' Warren frowned at her, his eyes concerned. 'Are we trying to do too much, Claire? Is that the trouble? Ben certainly thinks we are, and he isn't the first.'

'Ben?' Claire felt her face stiffen. 'He's been speaking to you?'

'From time to time and then yesterday when we met at the hospital.' Warren waved a hand as if to dismiss the significance of any such conversation. 'Over the years he's often suggested we ought to consider another partner. And with David—' He stopped abruptly, then went on, 'Well, David needs some time away for a while.' He lowered his head, seeming to muse on David's holiday. 'Martin's all right, but he hardly pulls his weight. Frankly, two or three days a week doesn't make much of a difference.'

Then he looked at her and frowned. 'Come, Claire,

you're not really so shocked, are you? You and Ben must have talked about it between yourselves.'

'Now and then.' She kept herself guarded. 'But I think we've been coping between the four of us.'

'That's what I thought,' Warren said, 'until lately. I thought I could manage to take on more but, knowing I haven't examined poor old Mr Coakes in so long...that's thrown me, Claire, and I don't mind admitting it. There's no excuse. How would you feel about it?'

'Another partner?' She blinked at him, still unnerved at hearing him talk about something he'd always opposed so adamantly. 'Full time, you mean?'

'Of course.'

'Is there enough work?'

'For two more, I should think.' Warren nodded. 'David needs his load lightened. Your workload is already high and you'll be away Thursdays from now on. I know that's only one day but there're holidays, and even with Martin asking for another day he'll cut them again when the children are at home. I can't help thinking that if we get more help with covering nights we'll be better during the days.'

He fixed her with his eyes. 'Think about it, Claire. Let me know. Obviously we can't decide anything while David's not here. We'll have a meeting when he gets back but, in the meantime, I'm open to suggestions. Goodness knows we could all do with half a day off each week.'

'I never thought I'd hear you say something like that,' she murmured, amazed.

'Circumstances change,' he said wryly. 'Perhaps I'm getting old.' He checked his watch, then briskly collected his medical bag. 'I should be out on my calls,' he told her. 'I'll drop in at the hospital on my way back and see how Reg Coakes is getting on.'

Claire cornered Martin after clinic and asked him if Warren had said anything to him about finding a new

partner, but Martin seemed as bemused as she'd been by
the suggestion.

'But it's a good idea,' he added. 'God knows how you
all put up with doing one in three on call. I did it for a
year and it almost killed me.'

'Two or three days a week doesn't leave you dissat-
isfied?' she asked, curious, for she'd never questioned
him about it before. 'You don't feel you're lacking con-
tinuity?'

'Sometimes,' he admitted heavily. 'But for the most
part I enjoy it and working more than that would take
too much of a toll on the kids.'

She hesitated. 'Would…do you think you and Prue
would still be together if it wasn't for the hours you both
worked?'

'To be frank, I'm not sure.' He didn't seem to mind
her questions. 'But we barely saw each other. It wasn't
a good life.'

'But now you're only working short shifts wouldn't
it work?'

'Prue's still in obstetrics,' he said wryly. 'Becoming
a consultant hasn't made much of a dent in her hours
and she tells me she's still called out most nights, only
now it's for her private patients.'

'She doesn't mind?'

'She loves it.' He looked a little forlorn. 'She used to
take the girls every second weekend at least, but this last
year they're lucky to see her once a month. Her career's
become so important to her that there's not much time
for anything else these days. I admire her dedication but
she's missing seeing the children grow up.'

On her way home late that night after a busy evening
on call Claire reflected on Martin's comments. None of
the things he'd said about Prue were true of her or Ben,
she decided. They both had jobs which were important
to them and both worked hard for long hours but for her,

and she was sure for Ben, too, Jamie remained the priority. Despite Ben's concern, she was confident that Jamie had never suffered because of her work. His comments about her neglecting him had been unfair. Jamie was a social child and obviously enjoyed spending time with other children and with his nannies after school, and she was confident that the variety of contacts was good for him.

She didn't feel as if she was missing out on seeing him grow up. There were times, of course, when she either couldn't get to school concerts and sports days or could only manage an hour or so there because of her work, but those occasions were infrequent and Jamie had never seemed to mind especially.

No, what bothered Jamie, she acknowledged again, was not her work, but the problems between her and Ben, problems that Ben seemed convinced could be magically solved by her spending a few more hours at home.

Which seemed grossly oversimplistic, she told herself wearily as she trudged towards the front door of the house. That made it doubly ironic that, given Warren's surprise comments that day, things seemed fated to fall Ben's way, regardless.

Her bleeper sounded as she was opening the front door, and she went directly to the telephone in the living-room and dialled her service. It was one of David's patients calling, an elderly woman who sounded extremely distressed. 'It's my husband, Doctor. I woke and found him lying on the floor in the bathroom. He's awake...but he can't get up and he can't seem to speak.'

'I'll be right there,' Claire soothed and took down the address, realising that it was only two streets from the house. 'Less than five minutes.' She asked the woman to turn on the outside light so that she'd recognise the flat more easily.

Ben came downstairs as she hurried to the door. 'Emergency?'

'Sounds like one of David's patients has had a stroke.' She pulled the door open. 'Did you meet Susan? Was Jamie happy with her? Do you think she'll be all right?'

'Yes, yes, and she seems very capable,' he said quietly, coming with her to the car.

She got in and unwound her window so she could talk to him as she started the engine. 'She'll be good, I think. She's very bright.'

'Wake me when you come home,' Ben said, bending to kiss her lightly.

'If I'm not too late,' she agreed, flustered by the memory of the night before. She waved him a brief farewell and accelerated out of the driveway.

But it was almost four before she arrived home again. Mr Adams's right side had been weak and he couldn't speak, confirming Claire's initial impression that he'd had a stroke, and the elderly-care registrar who'd admitted him had agreed. It would be at least twenty-four hours, though, before they could be confident of the diagnosis as sometimes the early symptoms resolved if the interruption to the affected brain's blood supply was not complete.

Arranging the ambulance and admission had been straightforward, but Mrs Adams had been too distressed to be left alone and as she had no relatives or close friends that she'd felt able to wake Claire had gone with her to the hospital then had taken her home again once her husband had settled and given her something to help her sleep.

Because it was so late she didn't wake Ben, as he'd suggested, but instead went straight to her own bed.

He left early the next morning and she only saw him for a few minutes. The following two days he was on call, covering for one of his colleagues, and apart from a brief exchange of greetings each morning she barely saw him as he returned each night after she was in bed.

The Thursday morning ENT clinic at the hospital wasn't as busy as it had been the week before and she finished early, but when she rang Ben to see if he wanted to meet for lunch his secretary informed her that he was delivering a lunchtime lecture. On a whim, Claire wandered through to the post-graduate centre. The lectures were a weekly event, hospital as well as visiting doctors featuring in the educational series, and she remembered that they occasionally managed to be entertaining.

Coffee and sandwiches were supplied and she helped herself to both from the trolley outside, before joining the doctors, medical students and other hospital staff thronging into the theatre for the talk.

She took a seat near the back of the hall, feeling anonymous within the large group, but Ben found her before he began speaking, and his questioning gaze brushed briefly over her still face as he commenced his lecture.

In keeping with a mixed audience the topic was broad, 'Transplant Surgery: What are our Limits?' Ben spoke well. It was years since she'd heard him like this and she'd forgotten how really good he was. Fluent yet dry, he spoke without notes, easily infecting his audience with his obvious fascination and understated excitement about changes in what was an otherwise specialised field.

Claire sat forward in her seat, not touching her sandwiches, and listened to the fluid, easy flow of his talk, mesmerised both by his words and by the unexpected glimpse of her husband's talents. He commanded his audience's attention and held it effortlessly, she noted. Instead of rustling lunch-bags and shifting cups there was a silence from the group, which she knew, from her junior doctor days, to be very rare.

He talked for forty minutes, using slides to illustrate his words, then spent the rest of the hour in open discussion, answering many of the audience's questions himself and directing others to his surgical colleagues.

At the end of the session, among the crowd as it slowly moved towards the exits, Claire listened with a vaguely disconcerting pride to the murmured comments around her about Ben's presentation.

'I'm going to come more often,' she heard a woman in a white coat just ahead of her say as they stalled on the steps. 'These talks used to be boring.'

Her companion chuckled. 'Be honest,' she whispered. 'It was more than the talk that held your attention.'

The first woman laughed. 'I suppose he's married?'

'According to the grapevine, very happily,' the other confirmed, making Claire blink. 'His wife's a doctor, too. A dermatologist.'

Dermatologist? Claire rolled her eyes, the grapevine's fallibility having been proved conclusively.

Ben was surrounded by doctors, including Lisa and his other juniors, and she'd intended to slip out of the door and meet him in Outpatients, but he looked up and caught her eye as she neared the door, then signalled for her to come down.

CHAPTER TEN

WITH a sigh of resignation Claire slipped around the crowd and made her way to the front. To her surprise, when she approached, Ben stepped away from the group, took her hand, leaned towards her and kissed her, briefly but with unmistakable possessiveness.

Out of the corner of her eye she saw Lisa scowl then stalk away, and Claire met Ben's calm gaze with a puzzled one of her own, wondering at the public gesture. He didn't comment, merely drawing her forward and towards a short, red-headed, lively-looking man in a dark suit. 'Claire, this is John Taylor, the new consultant on our team. He's taking over from Duncan. John, my wife Claire. I don't think you met at Duncan's retirement party.'

'No. No, we didn't. I was late as usual.' John Taylor grinned at her as he shook her hand. 'Pleased to meet you, Claire. You're as beautiful as the rumours.'

Claire flushed. 'I've just heard another rumour that Ben's wife is a dermatologist,' she said, tugging lightly to suggest he release the hand he still gripped. 'Perhaps he has a double life?'

'If so, I'll take the one with you in it,' he said fluidly, not releasing her.

'Back off, John.'

Ben's tone was dry but effective and the other man dropped her hand as if it had suddenly stung him. 'Teasing, Ben,' he said easily, his smile warm. 'Only teasing.' He tilted his head at her. 'Any sisters, Claire?'

'Only child. Sorry.' But she returned his smile, unoffended by his generous charm. 'Are you looking for a wife or a mistress?'

Something almost sad flashed across his face and she looked quickly at Ben but his expression told her nothing, and when John spoke a few seconds later his tone was cheerful again. 'Definitely a wife,' he told her. His eyes were sparkling once more, making her wonder if she'd imagined the other expression. 'The other would frighten me silly.'

She laughed and they chatted for a few minutes before Ben interrupted again, steering her away and explaining that they were due in clinic.

'John's wife died five years ago,' he told her briskly, when she questioned him about the other man. 'Lymphoma,' he said, referring to the cancer that develops in the cells of the lymph system. 'He's raising a young girl who's about the same age as Jamie. They've bought a house quite close to ours, Stamford Brook, I think. I thought we might invite them around next time we have a barbecue.'

'I'd like that. You know him quite well, then?'

'We trained together at King's,' he confirmed. 'He's been working in Canada for the last nine years, but with Duncan's retirement approaching I suggested he applied for the post.'

'I've never heard you talk about him.'

'It's work,' he said coolly. 'Not something we often discuss.'

His, she supposed he meant. Hers they seemed to discuss too often.

They were at Outpatients now and Lisa gave her a frosty look when they entered, before disappearing into one of the consulting rooms with a bundle of notes, but the other doctors, Mike and his house officer, both smiled a welcome.

'Claire, sit in with me this session,' Ben told her.

'Next week you can work on your own, once you get an idea of the sort of protocols I want used.'

Ben saw a mixture of new referrals and follow-ups of patients he'd seen before either in clinic or on the ward. With the new referrals she was impressed both by the calm and reassuring way in which he elicited histories of their complaints and with the skilled thoroughness of his examinations. His follow-up patients were obviously enthusiastic about the treatment they'd already received.

After clinic she went with him up to the ward to see Mr Coakes. Five days after his surgery he was now out of Intensive Care and they found him sitting in a chair beside a bed in one of the surgical wards. He looked tired but fairly well and he managed a smile for her when they exchanged greetings.

'I've been up for a walk with the physio,' he told them, indicating the Zimmer walking-frame at the end of his bed. 'Just to the end of the ward, though, at first.'

'It's a good start,' Ben told him. 'Well done.' He nodded to his SHO, who'd rushed to join them and was now hauling the curtains around the bed. 'No problems?'

'A few bugs in the urine, according to the sample sent yesterday, so Lisa told the nurses to take the catheter out,' Mike said, showing him a blue sheet of paper which looked to Claire like a microbiology result. 'No fever or other symptoms. He's using a bottle now without any difficulty and, aside from that, everything is progressing well. He managed some fluids this morning and we started him on fifty mils of fluid orally per hour this afternoon. Lisa said he could start free fluids tomorrow. Pulses are still excellent.'

'Good.' Ben's hands were at Mr Coakes's feet, clearly assessing the character of the pulses himself. Then he bent to examine the patient's bandaged abdomen, listened with his stethoscope and straightened.

'Start free fluids tonight,' he told Mike, adjusting Lisa's orders. 'Light breakfast tomorrow.'

'Food?' Mr Coakes brightened visibly. 'A pint of stout would do me a world of good.'

Claire saw the grin Ben was quick to hide. 'One tomorrow night, if you're up to it,' he said easily, scrawling a note on the bottom of the chart at the end of his bed. 'Might help get your strength back.'

'I need something with that physio of yours.' But Mr Coakes's eyes were twinkling now. 'Two, did you say?'

'One,' Ben said firmly, but Claire saw he was still amused. 'You're out of practice and we don't want you playing up for the nurses.'

'Now there's a thought.' He looked wistful. 'Thank you, Doctor. I appreciate it.'

'Keep up the walking,' Ben told him. 'At this rate we'll have you out of here in another week.'

'Thank you, too, Dr Marshall,' Mr Coakes said, squeezing the hand Claire had lowered to touch his. 'You've been very kind.'

'You're welcome,' Claire said quietly. 'I'm glad to see you looking so much better.'

Leaving Ben to the rest of his patients, Claire thanked him for the afternoon and rushed away for the evening clinic at the practice which she had to take since she was on call.

She was home late that night, Ben was on call on Friday and she didn't see him and then she was on call for the weekend. After breakfast on Saturday morning she went in to work as soon as Susan arrived, the younger woman happily having agreed to mind Jamie while Ben went to the hospital for the ward round he always held after a night on call.

It was another busy weekend and she saw little of Jamie or Ben over the two days. As Ben was on call on Monday and out at a college meeting on Tuesday and she was on call on Wednesday, it wasn't until the following Thursday afternoon when they met for lunch before his clinic that they had time for anything more than fleeting conversation.

'Susan's doing well,' she told him, as they munched hospital-issue egg and cress sandwiches out on a bench in the hospital grounds, enjoying some of the beautiful sunshine which had been obscured by clouds and drizzle during the past week. 'Jamie said he came first in his reading yesterday and he seems to be enjoying the extra homework his teacher's setting.'

'Because Susan rewards him with games.' Ben sent her a sideways look. 'Making it fun. Is she interested in teaching as a career?'

'She's still finding her feet.' Claire kicked off her shoes and leaned back against the bench, letting her eyes close. 'She's very bright but the past few years have been rough. I'm hoping that seeing Jamie do well will increase her confidence.'

'If it does we'll be looking for another child-minder again.'

Claire opened her eyes. 'Warren's talking about advertising for two more partners,' she said abruptly. 'I suppose we'll have a meeting about it when David gets back next week.'

'Surely David's not due back so soon?' Ben was watching a sparrow that was hopping at his feet for crumbs, not looking at her.

'He says Warren wants him to stay away longer, but he prefers to come back.' She took another mouthful of her sandwich, chewed slowly and then swallowed. 'He might take a week in winter to go skiing.'

'You've spoken to him?'

'A few times.' She stiffened at his sharp enquiry. 'He phones now and then to check on his patients.'

Ben sighed. 'Aren't you being rather naïve, Claire?'

'No.' Tense now and her appetite gone, she rewrapped her food and put it on the bench beside her. 'Aren't you being rather ridiculous?'

'If he's concerned about work matters why hasn't he called his locum?'

'He might have.'

'He hasn't.'

'How would you know?' She frowned at him. 'You don't even know her.'

'Warren told me. He thought none of you had heard from him since the Friday afternoon when he practically had to shove him out of the surgery to get him away from you.'

'What?' She spoke sharply. 'What are you talking about? When did Warren tell you that?'

'When we last spoke.' Ben met her regard with a calm that seemed entirely deliberate. 'Do you have a problem with me talking to him?'

'I have a problem with you discussing me behind my back,' she said carefully, determined to keep her voice level.

'We didn't discuss you.'

'You discussed David.'

'At some point,' he conceded.

'Why?'

'Why not?' Having finished his sandwich now and apparently unconcerned by her irritation, Ben collected the empty packet and stood, checking his watch. 'Time, Claire. Let's go.'

'You've no right to discuss him with Warren,' she said tightly, collecting her sandwich and stalking after him.

'Warren's worried about David's work.'

'Warren…?' Horrified that the older man knew anything about Ben's ridiculous assertions, she glared at him as she dumped her food into the bin he'd opened. 'What does Warren know about this?'

'What he sees.' Ben's mouth was tight. 'More than you, obviously.'

'And what's David's work got to do with you?'

'Nothing. But the fact that he thinks he's in love with my wife has something to do with me, don't you think?'

'No!' She stopped, appalled. 'Ben, you're wrong. How many times do I have to tell you that?'

'Is that why he telephones you when he's supposed to be on leave?' he said grimly, turning back to face her. 'Is that why he can't keep his eyes off you? Is that why virtually every time Warren sees him he's with you or looking for you or talking about you?'

'But that isn't true,' she protested.

'Wake up,' he said harshly.

'I am awake!'

'If I thought for one minute...' Ben's hand lifted to her throat, tilted her chin up to him and lingered, his eyes darkly unreadable. 'No,' he said finally, his grip relaxing. 'No I don't believe it. I'd see it.'

'See what?' She wrenched herself away. 'I don't understand you.'

'It's not complicated.' But his face had closed now and, although she was still bewildered, she knew he'd tell her nothing more. He took her hand and tugged her forward. 'We're late.'

Clinic was busy and afterwards he was called away to Theatre for an emergency so she went home alone. Although she tried to stay up she was tired and eventually was forced to go to bed before he came home.

The next morning she decided to probe Warren about the things he'd discussed with Ben but he seemed to be going out of his way to avoid her, and Claire wondered if Ben had said something to him. Regardless, he was impossible to pin down, always either too busy to be interrupted or on the telephone or out of the surgery every time she tried to find him.

She checked with David's locum, who confirmed that she'd not heard from David since starting the job, but Claire told herself that that meant nothing. In all likelihood David hadn't wanted to bother her unnecessarily when Claire could easily give him the information he wanted.

Saturday was warm. Ben had been late home the night before and she didn't see him until after his morning ward round when he arrived home while she and Jamie were enjoying a late breakfast in the garden.

'John was in at work,' he said, helping himself lazily to a piece of her toast as he sat beside them. 'He's thinking of driving to the Kent coast with his daughter this afternoon. He wanted to know if we're interested? Are we?'

'I haven't planned anything else,' she said slowly, brushing a crumb of bread from Jamie's eager face. She'd liked Ben's new colleague, and knew Jamie would enjoy the outing. It was several weeks since they'd been out together. It would be fun, especially with John and his daughter around to quell any tension. 'I'd like to go.'

'Me, too.' Jamie beamed. 'I can practise my swimming.'

'I'll call him.' Ben went inside. 'Picnic or restaurant for lunch?'

'Picnic, please.' She had some chicken and salad in the fridge and they'd be able to pick up more supplies on their way.

On such a lovely day the roads were crowded and they were half an hour late getting to the meeting spot they'd agreed, but John had had the same trouble with the traffic and he assured them that he and Katie had arrived only minutes earlier.

As she walked from the car park, swinging a picnic basket, Claire surveyed the broad expanse of beach beneath the chalky cliffs with pleasure, taking deep breaths of the ozone-scented air as they all trooped down towards the sea. Not too crowded, the beach and its small blue lapping waves looked inviting.

'Jamie, come back and get some cream,' she called

when he darted ahead. The sun was strong and she didn't want to risk him burning. 'Pull your hat down.'

'I'm going to teach Katie to swim,' he told her proudly, as he let her rub the sunblock into the pale skin of his back and chest, the two children already friends minutes after meeting. 'She's not very good. They never went to the sea in Canada.'

'I'll come with you.' She glanced at Ben, who was busy with John, setting up the shade umbrella, then kicked off her flip-flops, hauled her T-shirt over her head and undid her sarong to reveal the navy one-piece she wore beneath. 'Come on, Katie.' She took the little girl's shyly offered hand while Jamie ran on. 'Let's prove that girls can swim, too.'

Despite its welcoming appearance and the heat of the sun, the water was icy cold against her legs, and instead of diving in she hesitated in the shallows and watched while the children dashed in enthusiastically.

'Chicken.' Ben lifted her suddenly into the air and made her squeal. 'Your turn, Mummy.'

'Yes, Daddy.' Jamie paddled about, laughing his delight as Claire wiggled in Ben's arms as he waded out into the depths. 'Push her in.'

'Ben...please,' Claire pleaded with him.

'Please what?' His dancing eyes were wicked.

'It's too cold.'

'Then swim fast.' He was laughing at her as he dumped her into the frothy water. He followed her, catching her legs and pulling her under. When she rebounded, shrieking from the cold, he kissed her. 'It'll warm up when you move.'

She fought him and laughed when he kissed her again, then surfaced spluttering and wiping her eyes.

'Mummy, you're wet,' Jamie told her, beaming.

'What a surprise.' She mouthed something impolite at a grinning Ben when the children weren't looking.

John came down with a beach-ball and they played

with it for a while, then Ben stayed in the water to supervise the children while she and John walked back up the
beach to unpack the cool-boxes. Along with the chicken
and salad, she'd picked up bread and juice and grapes
and half a watermelon from the supermarket, and John
had brought salmon and a wedge of Brie along with a
cold bottle of Chardonnay to add to the feast she presented on a woven car-rug.

'Katie's enjoying herself,' John said, smiling at his
daughter's cries of laughter as she leapt through the
waves with Jamie. 'She's been quiet since we came back
to England. I've been worried about her.'

'She's bound to take time to settle in,' Claire said.
'New school, new friends, new country. All children
would take a while to adapt but at least when they do
they generally do it well.'

'I guess.' He watched Katie. 'It took a while for me
to adapt to Canada, I suppose. But coming home's been
surprisingly easy.'

'Were you out there for long?'

'Left here nine years ago come the first of next
month.' He grinned at her. 'Two months before you
must have started work with Ben. He was enjoying himself as a carefree bachelor the last time I saw him at my
wedding. I rang him ten weeks after I left and he told
me he'd found the woman he intended to marry. We
were stunned.' His regard was flattering. 'Of course, now
I've met you I understand the haste.'

'Two weeks after I started working for him?' Claire
frowned at him, the compliment passing almost over her
head. 'But we didn't decide to marry until…until at least
four months after that.'

'He must have made his decision a lot earlier,' John
told her. 'You know Ben doesn't stand back when he
sees something he wants.'

'But we must have only just met,' she protested.

'So he said.' John's grin widened at her expression.

'But I thought—' She stopped. She'd always thought they'd married because of Jamie. They'd been lovers but until she'd become pregnant he'd never talked about anything permanent.

'Well, I didn't think he thought that so quickly,' she murmured, swivelling on her knees to extract the picnic plates from the basket. So often these days it seemed that the longer she knew Ben the less she understood him. 'What else did he say about me?' she asked airily, pretending unconcern as she arranged the cutlery. 'In the beginning, I mean.'

'This and that.' Claire saw where Katie's mischievous smile came from. 'Ask him.'

'I will.' She waved at Ben to indicate that lunch was ready and smiled as he effortlessly plucked Jamie and Katie from the water, carrying one under each arm up the beach.

They stayed until around five. It was still hot and Claire could see that both Jamie's and Katie's noses were beginning to turn pink, despite all the sunblock and the shade of the umbrella for the few occasions when they ventured out of the water, so she suggested it was time to head back.

'Join the crowds,' John agreed, grimacing at the cars already forming a queue on the road. 'We must do this again.'

'We'd love that.' Claire smiled, meeting Ben's enigmatic regard briefly when John's hand clasped her bare shoulder and he kissed her sandy cheek. 'It's been a great day.'

Jamie was asleep before they joined the main road and Claire leaned back in her seat, watching Ben beneath her lashes. 'I like John,' she said. 'And Katie's lovely. That was fun.'

'Good.' His attention was on the busy road, and he didn't look at her.

'I didn't realise you were such good friends.'

'He moved to Canada shortly before you and I met.'

'He said...' She felt herself flushing. 'He said that you told him just after he got there that you were going to get married. But I worked out the dates. That must have been just after we met.'

'He's got a long memory.' The cars in front had their brake lights on and Ben slowed.

'You didn't tell me then.'

'Perhaps you weren't ready to know.' His sideways glance perused her face briefly, before returning to the traffic.

'So it's true?'

'I don't imagine he has any reason to make it up,' he replied blandly.

Claire sank her teeth into her lower lip, waiting until they were through the intersection that was delaying the traffic before she tried again. 'When did you decide you wanted to get married?'

'To get married?' Ben asked smoothly. 'Or to marry you?'

'Oh.' Her lashes fluttered down. Of course. John had not said that Ben had told him whom he wanted to marry. There'd been someone else. Someone whom he'd been in love with before her. It was hardly surprising, but it still shook her. 'Marry me,' she said miserably.

She felt rather than saw his eyes flicker across her face. 'About three days after I met you,' he said quietly.

Claire's head snapped up. 'What?'

'You were seeing a child in Casualty, a five-year-old with abdominal pain. I watched you examining her, and you were watching her and you were careful and gentle and your nose was wrinkled, the way it always is when you're concentrating hard, and I could see how determined you were to make the diagnosis. Then you looked up and saw me, but I could see that you didn't want me to spoil it for you. You wanted to decide yourself before I could interfere.'

'And that was it?' she said hoarsely, not even remembering the episode.

'And your hair was loose and the sun was coming through the window behind you, turning your blouse transparent,' he added quietly, his mouth quirking slightly as if at the memory. 'But I wasn't going to mention that.'

'And you decided you wanted to *marry* me?'

'About then.'

'I thought you only decided that with…with Jamie.'

'Did you?' His glance was enigmatic. 'Curious.'

'But that's the first time you mentioned anything about it.'

'Was it?' He braked smoothly for a car that cut ahead of him into their lane. 'It was a long time ago, Claire. Is any of this particularly important now?'

Very important, she realised. 'What if I hadn't been pregnant?' she said quickly. 'When would you have told me?'

'When I thought you were ready.'

'And when would that have been?'

'This is hypothetical,' he said calmly.

'But I want to know.'

'Does it make any difference?'

'To me, yes.'

'Not now, Claire.'

Behind her Jamie stirred, reinforcing Ben's command of caution, and Claire turned quickly to look at him, reassuring herself that he was still fast asleep. Knowing that she couldn't risk this conversation when Jamie might wake at any time, she bit her lip and looked searchingly at Ben. His eyes stayed on the road and he was clearly not about to volunteer any more information so, with a barely suppressed moue of frustration, she flicked on the radio, tuning it into a talk show with the vague idea that the discussion might distract her.

Jamie woke when they were just minutes from home,

but he was sleepy and grumpy and only stayed awake long enough to let her coax him into eating beans on toast and having a bath before he fell into bed.

Once she'd tucked him in Claire took a quick shower to wash away the sand that still clung to her skin and hair, then dressed in jeans and a light cotton jumper and went to find Ben.

The evening was warm and still sunny, and he'd opened the French doors wide and now sat just inside them on an armchair, studying the morning's *Independent* with a glass of white wine in his hand. Through the leaves of an ageing oak in the garden the sun played across his face, turning it from light to shadow and back to light again. The darkness of his hair suggested that he'd showered as well as changed while she'd been bathing Jamie, and in his jeans and casual shirt he looked powerful yet relaxed.

Finding herself oddly reluctant to disturb him, Claire hesitated in the living-room doorway, quiet, conscious of an ache deep inside her as she observed him. It was a feeling she often experienced when watching Jamie, a dull, gnawing, yet joyful, soft feeling that she knew was love. But with Ben there was a physical aspect to the feeling, a stark longing to be close to him that dominated all else.

She leaned back against the doorframe and closed her eyes, letting the feeling flood her.

While her recognition of her love might have dulled these last years, she knew the emotion itself was too familiar not to have been there all the time. When she'd wondered if her love had faltered the defect had only been superficial—she'd been preoccupied with the frustrations of day-to-day living, frustrations which had blinded her to the realities of her life. The reality of her life was Ben. It was as simple as that.

Her heart thumped as she finally let herself acknowledge the truth. Although she wanted Jamie to have his father, that was only a small part of why she was so desperate to preserve her marriage. The overwhelming reason was that she was still in love with her husband.

She must have said something, moved slightly—something—because Ben looked up sharply, directly at her. He folded the newspaper and stood. 'Wine?'

'Please.' Her voice sounded shaky, and her steps as she walked into the room were uneven.

'Let's sit outside.' His shadowed eyes probed hers as he passed her a glass of the chilled liquid. 'How's Jamie?'

'Sound asleep.' She was nervous. She walked ahead of him into the garden and to the white wrought-iron chairs still on the lawn from when they'd eaten breakfast that morning. 'I haven't organised anything for dinner,' she said stiffly, once she was seated.

'I'm not hungry.'

His steady regard flustered her. 'What John said today startled me,' she said huskily. 'I never realised you didn't just propose because…of Jamie.'

His expression didn't change. 'You knew I loved you.'

'I know you told me that,' she countered. 'And I know you did,' she added hastily when his brows drew together. 'But you're a responsible man and you wanted children and we were…compatible. I thought you must have decided it was the right time. I thought I was convenient.'

'What was convenient was that I wanted you.' He was watching her closely. 'You said you felt the same.'

'I did.' Flushing now, she spoke rapidly. 'I think I loved you almost from the first day I met you. I couldn't explain why or how but I saw you and something…shifted inside me.'

'You were inexperienced.'

'Sexually, yes,' she admitted, stiffening at his cool dismissal of her feelings, 'but I was an adult.' She stared at him when he remained silent. 'Didn't you believe I loved you?'

'I believed you believed it.'

'What does that mean?'

'Not a lot.' His mouth tightened. 'Leave it.'

'No.' She leaned forward and spread her arms palms up on the table. 'Ben, please, talk to me. I want to understand the way you feel. I want to understand what you're saying.'

'And then what?' Briefly his eyes probed hers but she knew the question was rhetorical and stayed silent. Ben looked away. He stretched his legs in front of him and crossed his ankles, but the relaxed pose was contrived, she sensed, for she could feel his tension like a shield around him and it made her tighten.

'You were working for me,' he said abruptly. 'You were innocent but I wasn't. I was experienced enough to make you feel any way I wanted you to. I took advantage of you and I made you pregnant.'

'Not…deliberately?' she asked hoarsely.

'Not the pregnancy,' he growled, capturing the hands that had clenched into fists in front of him, his grip cool but hard against her wrists. 'That was…poor control on my part,' he said harshly. 'I mean everything else. I deliberately set out to make you feel that way about me.'

'But that's so patronising.' She wrenched her hands away from his. 'And wrong. You can't *make* someone fall in love with you. I loved you for myself. And Jamie was my responsibility more than yours. I thought it was safe and I told you it was safe—even though you've never said anything, you must remember that. But then…when it happened I wanted him. I wanted him and I wanted to spend the rest of my life with you. I thought everything was perfect.'

'Perfection, by its nature, is illusive.' He sounded weary. He took a mouthful of his wine, and regarded her briefly over the rim of the glass. 'It was good, Claire. Never perfect.'

Never perfect. She jerked, her eyes wide. For her the first years had been sublime. But then she remembered that he'd said he'd *loved* her, not that he still loved her and not that his love had lasted any longer than those months before Jamie's birth.

She wanted to run away. She wanted to flee somewhere where those cool, thoughtful eyes couldn't observe her distress so calmly, but instead she gripped her seat, her fingers curling into the ironwork. Frank discussion between them these days was far too rare for her to take flight now, and she'd asked him for this. 'I thought it was perfect,' she said thickly. 'I was very happy. I didn't realise you weren't.'

'I wasn't unhappy,' he said, his words now tinged with impatience. 'How could I be? I had what I wanted.'

She shivered. 'Jamie.'

'Both of you. I never expected perfection, Claire. That was never part of the equation.'

'Then what was?' she demanded hoarsely.

His mouth tightened. 'Claire—'

'Please, Ben.'

'Sex,' he said abruptly. 'Loyalty. A partnership that I hoped would last until our children were adults.'

Her insides seemed to have frozen. 'I don't understand you,' she whispered, staring into the dark, guarded shadows that were his eyes. Appalled that those cold, clinical words described what he'd expected from their marriage, she could barely gasp out the words.

'I don't think I've ever understood you, not properly. I try to read you, try to work out what you're thinking, how you feel, but I've been wrong. I thought everything was fine until I went back to work properly. Then you told me that if I cut my hours everything would be better, and I started to let myself believe you. I thought we had had perfection, don't you see?' She was crying now, unable to stop the slow trickle of wetness on her cheeks, and with her hands curled into the chair as if it were a lifebuoy she couldn't even wipe them away.

'I thought that if both of us worked hard enough then we could find that again. I didn't realise you thought we didn't have anything worth saving.'

'Claire...?' She heard the scraping of his chair and then his arms were warm against hers, strong as they slid beneath her thighs, lifting her against him and forcing her grasping fingers to loosen.

'Don't cry,' he soothed, rocking her slightly as he carried her inside. 'God! I didn't mean to make you cry.'

She turned her face into his chest, feeling his shirt dampen with her tears. He took her to the armchair he'd abandoned earlier and sat, holding her in his arms. 'I thought everything was going to be all right,' she whispered between sobs. 'I thought it was...starting to work out. I thought...we'd been through the worst. I thought...the rest...was going to be easy.'

'I'm sorry.' Ben's hand brushed tear-damp hair from her eyes and tucked it behind her ears, his eyes so warm with concern that her sobs started anew. 'Claire, I'm so sorry.'

'Is it Lisa?' she asked painfully. 'Or other women? Did I ever satisfy you?'

'There's no one else.' His mouth brushed her forehead, kissed her. 'Never. It's not that, nothing to do with that. Shh,' he murmured, his thumb gentle at her cheeks as he captured the moisture. 'Hush. Don't cry.'

'I can't live like that,' she told him later, when the tears finally stilled. 'Not knowing it's for that. Not just for sex and trying to be loyal and waiting until Jamie's grown up. I'm sorry, Ben. Even for Jamie, I just can't. It'd kill me.'

Although they were close, his arms gentle around her, she realised she'd never felt more isolated.

After a long, desolate silence Ben said quietly, 'The

house is yours.' So matter of fact that she realised he'd merely been waiting for her to voice the words he continued, 'And the shares and the money in the joint accounts.' He kissed her so gently she felt the tears collecting again. 'I'll organise an allowance for Jamie.'

'What will you do?'

He stroked her hair, his eyes watching the movement of his hand. 'I can stay at the hospital till I find somewhere else.'

'No.' She touched his face. 'Stay here,' she whispered, sobbing softly. 'Till you find somewhere properly to live, somewhere nice. I can't bear to think of you in one of those little rooms.'

'All right.' Her fingers had dropped to his mouth and now he kissed them, making her gasp with the pain of remembered passion.

'What will we tell Jamie?'

'Nothing till everything's sorted. Then we'll tell him the truth. We'll explain that he'll always have both of us, that we love him.'

Her eyes filled anew. 'I'm sorry, Ben.'

'I know.' He lifted her again. 'You're tired,' he said gently, carrying her upstairs to her room. 'Get some sleep. I'm going into the hospital for a few hours. Will you be all right?'

'I don't know,' she said dully, when he lowered her to her bed. She didn't feel as if she'd be all right ever again. She turned on her side, away from him, and seconds later she heard him walk away.

CHAPTER ELEVEN

CLAIRE managed to get through Sunday by feigning a superficial cheerfulness, apparently good enough to fool Jamie. Ben was out all day and arrived home as she was preparing for bed, but he didn't come in to see her.

On Monday morning she heard him leave around six, and when she got up Jamie told her that he'd said he would be working late that night.

David was back. His car was in the car park, and when she was making herself a strong coffee to get through her morning clinic he came into the kitchen, his face drained and tense, looking even worse than he had before his holiday.

'I need one of those,' he said tightly, holding out a mug for her to fill with some of the drink she'd brewed. 'Hi, Claire. Great to be back. Good holiday. Missed you all. Ready for work.'

She registered the fake heartiness and the way his hand trembled as he lifted the cup, and looked at him searchingly, noting the bloodshot eyes and exaggerated confidence. He looked as if he hadn't slept the whole time he'd been away. He looked, she noted worriedly, even worse than she. 'David...?'

'Can't stop,' he said abruptly. 'Warren's on the warpath. If he catches this little tête-à-tête I'm in for another blasting. Notice how hard he works to keep me away from you?'

She followed him to the door. 'What are you talking about?'

'You don't know?' His lip curled. 'Ask your husband,' he rasped, his eyes sliding away from her as he walked into his office. 'He gave the orders.'

Claire froze. 'What's Ben got to do with anything?' she said shakily.

'Everything.' David closed the door firmly in her face.

Her morning clinic was busy and finished late, and she had to rush out for her calls directly after she'd shown out her last patient so she had no time to talk to either Warren or David to try and make sense of his odd accusation.

One of the patients on her list, an elderly man with chronic bronchitis who needed antibiotics for a chest infection, lived next door to Mr Coakes, newly discharged after his aneurysm repair. After seeing her patient, Claire came out of the house to find him hobbling around his garden, a fluffy grey cat at his feet.

'Checking on Jack's vegetables,' he told her. 'He has a hard time getting down to do the work.'

'The tomatoes look healthy,' she commented, bending to scratch under the purring cat's chin. Although still green, the fruit was plentiful. 'He's going to have a good crop.'

She studied him, pleased that he was looking relatively fit but worried by how much work he must be doing. Jack Timmins was on oxygen sixteen hours a day and largely housebound, and she suspected that most of the immaculate garden's care fell to Mr Coakes.

'Are you sure you're fit enough for this? You haven't been out of hospital long. I'm surprised you can bend.'

'I'm just looking to see what needs doing,' he reassured her. 'The lassie on the other side's been coming in to help with most of it, and my neighbour's helped, too, in return for some vegetables for herself. Your husband tells me it'll be six months before I'm back to normal activities so until I'm better I'm just supervising both of them,' he added, lively blue eyes twinkling at her. 'Enjoying it, too.'

'I'm sure you are.' She smiled, stepping over the cat which had now twined herself around her ankles. 'Your own garden's looking beautiful. Your roses are gorgeous.'

'Hard work but it's worth it,' he acknowledged. 'Are you a gardener yourself, Dr Marshall?'

'I used to be,' she said ruefully. 'Sadly I don't have time these days.'

'It's hard when you're busy.' He and his cat walked her to her car. 'But worth making time, I think. A garden gives back twice what you put into it and there's nothing like the taste of home-grown vegetables.'

'We're used to supermarket ones now,' she said lightly, bending again to stroke the friendly cat before opening the Audi's boot to deposit her medical bag.

'I'll bring in a few pounds of tomatoes when they've ripened,' he told her as she walked around to the driver's door. 'For you and Mr Howard. That'll change your mind.'

'I'd like that,' she said, with a smile that faltered when she realised that Ben wouldn't be with her come summer.

Both Warren and David proved elusive that afternoon, and David was out on a call and Warren still busy with a patient when the time came to leave the surgery.

Aside from a brief, impersonal exchange of greetings the next morning she still couldn't corner either of them, but early on Tuesday evening, running late for her teaching session after becoming mercifully engrossed in some paperwork she was finishing, she was preparing to leave when she heard David's raised voice coming from his office. She lifted her head, stiffening as she heard Warren shout something back. The words were muffled and indistinguishable but his tone was definitely angry, and David's reply equally so.

Cautiously she opened her door. It made the voices louder but still she couldn't make out the words. The surgery had once been a sturdy house—brick-walled and solidly insulated, the rooms were almost sound-proof.

Then, abruptly, David's door opened and, not wanting either of them to see her there and discover she'd been eavesdropping, she slid back into her room and pulled her own door gently shut.

'David, be reasonable,' she heard Warren say in a low voice, as if he didn't want to be overheard. 'Think about this—'

'Stay away from me,' David warned. 'If you say anything to Claire I swear I'll go straight to the authority.'

'David...?'

'You can't force me to do anything,' David stormed, and Claire heard the surgery's back door open then slam closed, followed by steps on the gravel outside.

For a few seconds she hesitated, then she hauled her door open and went after them. Her name had been mentioned and, as far as she was concerned, she had a right to know what was going on. She was almost at the back door when she heard the sound of a car being driven at speed into the car park. Through the glass panels of the door she caught sight of its driver and froze.

Ben, his face like thunder, leapt out, and David's clearly horrified expression when he saw him made Claire pale. She stood numbly and stared outside, watching as Ben made purposefully for the younger man who'd started to back away but now had come hard up against Warren's car.

Warren was talking and lifting his arms, looking as if he was pleading for something, but she couldn't hear the words—only David's shout of fury as Ben grabbed at his shoulders and shook him.

Mobilised by real fear that David would get hurt, Claire wrenched the door open. 'What on earth is going on?' she screamed at Ben, her gaze clinging hungrily to him. 'Are you mad?'

They turned, all of them, their faces equally shocked.

Ben recovered first. His arms dropped and he stepped back from David. 'Your car's not here,' he said harshly. 'You're supposed to be at the university tonight.'

'I'm running late,' she said distantly. 'I left my car on the street because someone was in my space when I got back from a call.'

'Claire, I'm sorry.' Warren looked the most disturbed. He shifted his feet, avoided her eyes. 'We all thought you'd gone. We wouldn't have...'

'Wouldn't have what?' she demanded when he faltered.

'It's not how it looks,' David said, his face still flushed. 'We were just...discussing something.'

'You were fighting,' she cried. 'Like schoolboys.' She glared at Ben accusingly. He was bigger and more powerful than David—it would have been no contest. 'How dare you do this!'

'It's not what you think.' Warren was watching David. 'Tell her.'

'There's nothing to tell,' David protested, his defensive tone—considering that he was the victim—making her frown.

'Tell her,' Warren repeated, harshly now. 'For God's sake, David. Are you that pathetic?'

The two men's eyes locked and after a few seconds David's dropped. His shoulders sagged. He mumbled something.

'What?' Warren was relentless. 'What did you say?'

'I have a drinking problem,' David said angrily, looking across to Claire. 'Claire, I have a drinking problem.'

'No.' She frowned, bewildered. 'I don't believe you.'

'It's true.' His voice dropped. 'God knows I wish it wasn't.'

Claire just stared at him, little things she'd noticed beginning to make a horrible sort of sense, but automatically she protested. 'You've been under a lot of strain lately.' She was talking quickly. 'Rebecca. Work. It's not surprising you're a little run down.'

'Claire, I'm an alcoholic!'

She sagged. 'Are you…are you having treatment?'

'I was.' He lifted his head. 'Stopped Friday at five. Started drinking Friday at five-thirty.'

Claire looked at Ben. He was very still, his expression guarded. 'You knew this?'

'Ben suspected it first.' Warren spoke instead. 'He came to me. We confronted him and tried to help, and when that didn't work we arranged for him to be admitted to a private unit in Surrey for detox. David—'

'I didn't want you to know,' David said. 'I didn't accept I had a problem—I just thought I needed time. I told them that if you were told anything I'd refuse to go along with any treatment.'

She felt awful that he hadn't felt he could come to her. 'Why?'

'I was ashamed.' His head dropped. 'Rebecca didn't know either. She suspected,' he admitted. He sent a quick look in Ben's direction. 'She spoke to Ben a few times but she didn't really know how bad it was.'

'So…this has been going on a long time,' Claire ventured.

'Two, three years,' David said flatly. 'Worse since Rebecca left.'

Claire felt helpless. She'd been there for him to talk with but that hadn't been enough. 'I'm sorry.'

'No one's fault.' His mouth turned down. 'Except mine, that is.'

'What's going on now?'

'I realised he'd been drinking again,' Warren told her. 'He was supposed to stay at least three weeks, preferably longer, at the clinic. When Ben warned me on Thursday that you'd said he was coming back this week I knew he must be discharging himself. Today we decided to have another go at forcing him to go back and try again.'

'And your work?' she said huskily, studying David, still stunned that so much could have happened without her realising. She hadn't been much of a friend, she thought, sick with guilt at the realisation that she'd been too preoccupied with her own problems to pay much attention to David these last months. If she'd spent more time with him, talked more, perhaps...

'No problems with his work,' Warren said firmly, before the younger man could speak. 'He's more responsible than to drink on duty, thank God.'

David winced. 'The health authority knew there was a...difficulty,' he admitted, his eyes on Claire. 'Warren had to inform them. They agreed I could continue working under supervision. Warren supervised.'

'So what's going to happen now?'

David's gaze flickered to Ben, then to Warren and back to her. 'I'm having trouble keeping myself together,' he said thickly. 'I need help.'

Claire saw Warren's shoulders sag, as if with relief, and she realised that was probably an admission David hadn't made before. 'Will you go back to the clinic?' she asked.

'I'll finish the course.' David leaned back against Warren's car and hung his head, obviously exhausted. 'Can you get someone to cover three months?'

'Katie's happy to cover short term and we'll look for two new partners,' Warren said, relieved, his hand briefly clasping the younger man's shoulder. 'We all need some of the pressure easing. By the time you get back we should have it sorted.'

'I'm sorry, Claire.' David lifted his head again and the small movement seemed difficult. 'Sorry for everything. I've caused trouble for you.'

'It wasn't you, David.' Glancing towards Ben's implacable expression, she suddenly found herself on the brink of tears. 'I'm only sorry I haven't been any help to you over this. We just want you well again and back with us. As soon as you can.'

'I'll do my best.' He managed a pale smile. 'I'm supposed to be covering your call tonight.'

'I'll stay.' Claire could hardly believe he was concerned about something so trivial. 'You mustn't worry.'

'I'll run you home.' A relieved-looking Warren opened his car door so David could climb in. 'Thanks, Ben,' he said in gratitude, nodding towards him. 'Appreciate the help.'

Ben nodded in acknowledgement and returned to his own car, which was still parked carelessly across the exit.

Claire watched forlornly as he started the engine, but rather than leave he moved forward into a space, lifting his hand as Warren and David drove out. He climbed out of the car and came towards her.

'David, tonight,' she said huskily, moving back into the surgery. 'Do you think he'll be all right?'

'Warren will drive him back to the clinic,' he said coolly. 'If you explain the basics I'll stay here and cover the surgery until after your teaching.'

'I don't mind staying,' she said mechanically, leading him through into the kitchen after checking with the receptionist on duty that there was no one waiting to see her and no urgent calls.

'So many secrets,' she mused, filling the kettle with water. 'What else don't I know?'

'I had no choice,' he said quietly.

'How did you find out?'

'Rebecca dropped a few hints. Then the day after your Christmas party here last year he rang me at the hospital. He was obviously drunk.'

Claire frowned. She remembered the party. Drinks and snacks after work. They'd all had a few glasses of champagne. Ben hadn't come because he'd been busy at the hospital. 'What did he say?'

'That he'd been kissing you.'

'But it was Christmas,' she protested. 'I don't even remember kissing him, but if I did it would have just been a peck on the cheek. Why would he tell you that?'

Ben hesitated and she could see he was reluctant to tell her, but finally he said briskly, 'He pretended to be a stranger and put on an accent, although it was obvious who he was. He told me that he'd seen him and you kissing—that you were having an affair. He said you were in love with him.'

'But that's ridiculous,' she said passionately.

'I knew that.' Ben's shrug was dismissive and she felt guilty anew about her suspicions concerning Lisa. If Lisa had rung her with such a story she was sickeningly aware that she'd probably have believed it.

'I told him to stay away from you and I told him he was sick,' Ben continued. 'That he needed help. He hung up.'

'And you told Warren?'

'I was worried about him,' he confirmed. 'Particularly about his work. I had to do something. Warren had been worried himself. David's clinical standards were high, but everything else was slipping. He'd been having minor problems—gastritis, headaches and so on—which fitted the diagnosis. Warren insisted David had a blood test and it showed disturbed liver function. We tried to persuade him to get treatment, but he was stuck in denial and refused to admit he had a problem. Outside just now is the first time he's admitted anything.'

'And that night you saw him…with me in the car park?'

'I rang him from Duncan's farewell and told him if I caught him near you again I'd kill him. I called Warren, told him everything and he arranged the clinic. Warren's pressure, together with my threats, forced him into agreeing to go.'

'But, unless he was willing, no one would have been able to help him,' she said faintly, pouring their coffee.

'We didn't know what else to do,' Ben admitted. 'The soft approach hadn't worked. We had to try the tough.'

'It sounds like he's decided he wants help now.'

'I hope so.' Ben took a mouthful of coffee. 'Warren says he's a good GP.'

'Very good,' she confirmed. 'Just…confused. Rebecca leaving really knocked him hard. He probably needs professional help to come to terms with that, too.'

'The clinic's set up for that,' Ben told her. 'The director's a psychiatrist, and the programme is holistically based.' He tilted his head. 'You're upset I didn't tell you.'

'I understand your reasons.' She sat at the table, and stared down at her drink. 'The crazy thing is that at first when I saw you about to grab him I was…excited,' she said faintly. 'I didn't want David hurt but for a few minutes I thought you were fighting him because you were jealous.' She couldn't look at him. 'Jealous of me.'

'You wanted that?' he said quietly, curiously almost.

'For a few seconds.' She hung her head, clutched her cup. 'Stupid, isn't it?'

'Stupid because nothing ever happened between you and David?'

'Because you don't want me.'

'Is that how I've behaved?'

'You're leaving.' She lifted her gaze but couldn't look at his face, focusing instead on the long finger that bore the wedding ring she'd given him. 'You never felt the same as I did. How was it that you put it? You wanted sex and loyalty and to be good parents?'

'I asked you once what you wanted and you said you thought the most important thing was to be good parents.'

She looked up, blinking. She *had* said something like that, she remembered, that night they'd made love in the kitchen. The memory of what had happened there made her flush. 'I didn't say that that was *all* I wanted,' she murmured.

'Then what else?'

'Much more than you. Perhaps I didn't fully understand what when I said that, but what I've always wanted is for you to love me like I love you.' She dared another look, saw his stillness and rushed on, her pride less important now than making him understand how she felt.

'You're my world, Ben. I love you so badly I ache when I look at you.' She took a deep breath, and lowered her head again. 'I want sex, of course, but if you were suddenly...impotent or paralysed I'd still love you. I want loyalty, but when I thought you were involved with Lisa I was ready to forgive you. I want us to raise Jamie together, but if we'd never had a child I wouldn't love you any less.'

She shook her head sadly. 'I know I said that staying together the way you feel would kill me, but I really have no idea how I'm going to manage without you. I'll cope, of course, for Jamie. But I'll never stop loving you.' She sniffed. 'Stupid, hmm?'

'Are you asking me to stay?'

'No.' She pushed her drink away. 'Not against your will. I'm not trying to make you feel guilty or concerned. I just want to tell you. So you know. Perhaps, in a few years, a little bit of you will remember this time kindly.'

'God, Claire!' She looked up to see him lowering his head to his hands. 'You don't have to make me feel guilty,' he muttered. 'I've felt guilty for years. What I said Saturday night was true. I forced you into marrying me in the first place. You were so young...still at the beginning of your career. You didn't stand a chance.'

'I didn't want a chance,' she protested. 'You must know that. I told you I loved you.'

'I meant to give you time—time to find yourself, time

to decide what you wanted to do with your life and your career, without me influencing you.'

'I knew where I was. I didn't need time. I wanted you to influence me.'

'You know how I felt when you told me about the baby?' he demanded. 'Glad,' he said harshly, when she shook her head. 'Fiercely, violently glad.'

'Because you wanted children.'

His eyes darkened. 'Because I wanted you.'

Claire swallowed heavily. 'You already had me.'

'Not the way I wanted.'

'As your wife?'

'As my wife. My lover. Exclusively. Where no other man could touch you. Where you could never escape.'

'That's the same way I wanted you,' she whispered, stunned by his admission. He'd been passionate, almost violently passionate in bed, but never outside of it. This raw, uncensored sharing of his emotions left her breathless.

'I thought it would dull,' he rasped. 'I thought after a few years I'd become more civilised.'

'You did,' she countered, paling as she thought about the last year especially.

'Nothing changed.'

'But you barely touched me.'

'I was determined to give you more space,' he said, taking one of her hands that twisted desperately on the table, holding it between his. 'Inside was still primitive. I wanted you home, in my bed, preferably pregnant, but suddenly you wanted your career back and I knew that if I didn't stand back and let you do what you wanted then I'd lose you.'

She opened her mouth to protest but he raised his hand to stop her. 'I thought we could adjust to things, but it wasn't that simple. You were working every hour under the sun, I barely saw you, you were making yourself ill from tiredness but you refused to admit it and we were sleeping in separate beds. I tried to hold back, give you room to decide if that made you happier than I could, but inside I was going mad. Most of the time I just wanted to throw you over my shoulder and take you to bed, but I knew I had to fight that.'

'No, you didn't.' She felt heady. 'I didn't object when you finally did.'

'I couldn't wait any longer,' he said thickly. 'At the beginning I left you alone because I thought you wanted space, and, God knows, I hadn't given you any before. When it became months I was stubborn. I wanted you to come to me. I'd thought that the sex had been as good for you as it had been for me but you seemed indifferent, and I thought I'd been wrong. You were driving me mad but I wanted you to want me as desperately as I wanted you.'

Suddenly those times when he'd rejected her tentative approaches made an awful sense. If she'd been more confident, more direct, he'd have responded to her. 'You wanted me to beg?'

'Yes!' His eyes were violent but unrepentant. 'Of course.'

'I was too shy,' she whispered. 'I missed you so desperately but you were so cold.'

'Not inside. Inside I was angry,' he said tightly. 'Seeing David kiss you was like a kick in the stomach. I wasn't jealous—I knew that he was desperately clutching at straws—but I felt primitive. I wanted to brand you, force you to admit that only I could give you pleasure.'

'You're the only one who ever has.' Her hand lifted to stroke the faint roughness of his cheeks. She felt as if she was drowning in the molten fire in his eyes. 'I was so jealous of Lisa.'

'I didn't realise at first. Later I was angry that you doubted me.'

'But you enjoyed it.'

'In a sick way,' he admitted flatly. 'How could you

have believed I'd touch her?' He sounded disgusted. 'I haven't looked at another woman since that day I saw you with that child in A and E. Nine years and I still don't see anyone else.'

'It's the same with me.' She moistened her lower lip, gazing at him in wonderment. 'Ben, there were reasons I thought you were involved with her. Jamie seemed to know her so well. He said he used to see her when he went into your office on weekends.'

'Probably.' He lifted one shoulder carelessly. 'We work closely together. If it's been a long night on duty and she and the juniors haven't had much sleep I sometimes take them to McDonald's for breakfast Saturday morning. Jamie comes along when you're working.'

'And you sometimes take her out in the evening?'

At his frown, she flushed. 'David said he saw you together at La Cantina one night.'

'Along with Mike and a couple of house officers,' Ben confirmed. 'A reward for a horrendous week.' His eyes darkened. 'He implied we were alone?' At her silence, he swore. 'He could hardly walk that night. He knew I was on to him and he was running scared. Probably stirring trouble was his misguided attempt at revenge.'

'Do you think it was all for that?'

'No.' Ben's lips compressed. 'The fact that he was so adamant you weren't told anything suggests that some of his feelings for you were real. Wasted, perhaps, but real.'

Claire closed her eyes briefly. 'He's been so unhappy.'

'He's a big boy,' he said, without sympathy. 'He'll get over it.'

'Were you ever jealous of him?'

'The hours you were working, there must have been times when you saw more of him than me,' he acknowledged. 'I worried more that you were too supportive when he needed to be confronted, but you didn't know the facts so I couldn't expect anything else of you. I wasn't seriously worried that you were attracted to him.'

'You practically accused me of that.'

'I was frustrated,' he said tightly. 'David was going off the rails, you and I were in trouble, and I had to keep things from you and there was nothing I could do about it. Staying quiet was too much for me at times, and even though I was determined not to complain about your work or your hours some complaint would often burst out anyway and we'd end up arguing. I've discovered I don't react well to frustration.'

'Neither do I.' She smiled hesitantly. 'Ben, I love you. I love you just as I always have, with all my heart.'

'Oh, Claire. I love you, too. God!' He shoved his chair back, caught her in his arms, swung her around and kissed her. 'I adore you. I can't believe you've ever doubted that.'

'I did. I thought you'd never really loved me,' she cried, kissing his face when he lifted her—his eyes, his cheeks, his wonderful, beautiful mouth. 'I thought when you said those things on Saturday that that was *all* you felt. I thought our whole marriage had been a lie.'

'I was trying to stay rational,' Ben murmured against her throat.

'I didn't want rational,' she whispered. 'I wanted passion.'

'I'd given you passion.' His mouth tracked to her ear...kissed her. 'It hadn't made any difference.'

'I wanted you to tell me it had been perfect.'

'In all the important ways it had been.'

She wrenched her head back and stared up at him. 'But...?'

'The guilt hasn't been easy,' he said softly. 'I always wondered what you would have done if I hadn't seduced you.'

'For the last time, you *didn't* seduce me,' she insisted, her voice rising. 'If you hadn't touched me I would have jumped on you. Eventually. I was in love with you. I have been deliriously happy with you. *Nothing* could have been better than that. Nothing.'

He groaned. 'I believe you,' he muttered, holding her against him so she could feel his desire, his arms hard around her.

'If only you'd told me how you felt years ago,' she said weakly. 'It's as if there's been a curtain between us.'

'You've drawn it back.' He lowered his mouth to her throat again, his hands at her thighs. 'Starting now, we discuss everything. Have you any idea how much I want you right now?'

'A little,' she said huskily, laughing softly at his urgency. 'Were you really going to leave me?'

'For a little while.' His hands gripped her hips when she twisted against him. 'As long as I could manage without trying to convince you to try again. In my current state that would have been an hour or two at most.'

'In my state it would have taken five minutes to beg you to come back.' She laughed as he kissed her.

'Ten seconds for me to accept.' He opened her mouth, his hands at her blouse. 'Make that five seconds.'

'Ben, no.' She captured his fingers. 'My receptionist…'

He put her down abruptly and swore. 'When do you finish?'

'I can be home by nine.'

'But you're on call?'

'And tomorrow,' she said weakly, her eyelids fluttering down as his hands briefly covered her cotton-shielded breasts. 'It'll be better when we get our new partners. I'll only be on call once a week, sometimes not at all.'

He stilled. 'You don't mind about more partners?'

'No.' She shook her head, catching her breath when he pulled her against him again. 'You were right, but I was too angry with you to see that. I thought you wanted me to give up my work so your life would become easier—'

'It wasn't like that.'

'I know that now.' She touched his face. 'You were worried about it taking too much out of me, and you were right. There's a difference between working full time and working all the time, but I just didn't see it. Even one more partner will take pressure off us, and seeing David the way he was today brings home to me how much we all need that.'

'Thank God for that.'

'Ben, I want another baby.'

'Just say the word.' His eyes turned lazily wicked.

'No, you can't.' She backed away, hands outstretched, but he was too quick for her, picking her up and slinging over his shoulder before she had time to draw breath. She squealed as he carried her out of the kitchen, her voice hoarse with urgency. 'Not now. Not here.'

'I'm just taking you to your office,' he said softly. 'Why, Dr Marshall, whatever were you imagining?'

'With you, Mr Howard, I will always be suspicious,' she said happily, kissing him as he lowered her to the floor beside her desk. 'But I adore you, anyway. Passionately.'

'We'll see how passionately after your clinic,' he said fervently. He kissed her cheek, a chaste, businesslike kiss. 'Hurry home, my darling. We'll be waiting for you.'

Claire looked after him, all the anxiety of the past year dispelled. 'Everything's going to be all right now,' she said wondrously.

Ben smiled, a warm, tender, loving smile. 'Everything is going to be perfect.'

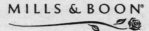

MILLS & BOON®

Sizzle

Soak up the sun with the perfect summer read

Four sizzling short stories in one volume— perfect for lazing on the beach or in the garden.

A combination of young, fresh, talented authors led by Jennifer Crusie—one of our most popular Temptation® writers.

Look out for Sizzle in August 1998 by Jennifer Crusie, Carrie Alexander, Ellen Rogers and Annie Sims

Available from most branches of WH Smith, John Menzies, Martins, Tesco, Asda, Volume One, Sainsbury and Safeway

MILLS & BOON®

Penny Jordan

COLLECTOR'S EDITION

Mills & Boon® are proud to bring back a collection of best-selling titles from Penny Jordan—one of the world's best-loved romance authors.

Each book is presented in beautifully matching volumes, with specially commissioned illustrations and presented as one precious collection.

Two titles every month at £3.10 each.

4 FREE

books and a surprise gift!

We would like to take this opportunity to thank you for reading this Mills & Boon® book by offering you the chance to take FOUR more specially selected titles from the Medical Romance™ series absolutely FREE! We're also making this offer to introduce you to the benefits of the Reader Service™—

- ★ FREE home delivery
- ★ FREE gifts and competitions
- ★ FREE monthly newsletter
- ★ Books available before they're in the shops
- ★ Exclusive Reader Service discounts

Accepting these FREE books and gift places you under no obligation to buy, you may cancel at any time, even after receiving your free shipment. Simply complete your details below and return the entire page to the address below. ***You don't even need a stamp!***

YES! Please send me 4 free Medical Romance books and a surprise gift. I understand that unless you hear from me, I will receive 4 superb new titles every month for just £2.30 each, postage and packing free. I am under no obligation to purchase any books and may cancel my subscription at any time. The free books and gift will be mine to keep in any case.

M8YE

Ms/Mrs/Miss/Mr.................................Initials ....
BLOCK CAPITALS PLEASE

Surname ....

Address ....

....

....Postcode...............................

Send this whole page to:
THE READER SERVICE, FREEPOST, CROYDON, CR9 3WZ
(Eire readers please send coupon to: P.O. BOX 4546, DUBLIN 24.)